She's turning into a vampire. . . .

"I don't want to be like Volker," Talli whispered. "Don't let me be a monster."

"I won't. I don't know what to do," Chris said, "but I promise I'll find out."

"I believe I might be of some assistance there," said a voice.

His hands still linked with Talli's, Chris twisted around to see a slim man in a long trench coat step from the shadows under the trees. Despite the calm expression on the man's face, there was something menacing about him as he advanced toward them.

"Stay back," Chris shouted.

"If I stay back," said the stranger, "then how can I help?" Moonlight played along his teeth as his lips parted in a wide smile. Behind him, Chris saw another figure moving through the shadows.

"Who are you?" Chris asked. He started to step forward, but Talli pulled him back.

"No, Chris, don't. It's Them."

"It's who?" asked Chris.

"I believe she means we are vampires," said the smiling man. "And she's quite right."

Don't miss the other two books in this
terrifying trilogy:

The Principal
The Substitute

Read these thrillers
from HarperPaperbacks!

Baby-sitter's Nightmare
Baby-sitter's Nightmare II
Sweet Dreams
Sweetheart
Teen Idol
Running Scared
by Kate Daniel

And look for

Love You to Death
Class Trip
by Bebe Faas Rice

THE
COACH

M. C. Sumner

HarperPaperbacks
A Division of HarperCollins*Publishers*

This is a work of fiction. The characters, incidents, and
dialogues are products of the author's imagination and are not
to be construed as real. Any resemblance to actual events or
persons, living or dead, is entirely coincidental.

HarperPaperbacks *A Division of* HarperCollins*Publishers*
10 East 53rd Street, New York, N.Y. 10022

Produced by Daniel Weiss Associates, Inc., 33 West 17th Street,
New York, New York 10011.

First printing: June 1994

Printed in the United States of America

HarperPaperbacks and colophon are trademarks of
HarperCollins*Publishers*

10 9 8 7 6 5 4 3 2 1

For John, who always likes his coaches.

With gratitude to the Alternate Historians: Tom Drennan, Valerie Gaston, Laurell K. Hamilton, Deborah Millitello, Marella Sands, Janni Simner, and Robert Sheaff. And to the Tale Spinners: John C. Bunnell, Kate Daniel, Karawynn Long, Mark Kreighbaum, Dan Perez, Sherwood Smith, and Kathleen Woodbury. It shouldn't take all these people to nurse me through one book, but it does. Thanks, folks.

THE
COACH

One

꧁꧂

Monday

The policeman's grip on his shoulder was a little too tight to be friendly.

Chris looked to the left as the officer steered him down a narrow hallway. They passed several windows made of security glass, the kind with crisscrossing wires worked into it. Through the windows Chris could see a large room where other police officers stood, or sat at paper-strewn desks.

Heads turned as Chris passed, and eyes followed his movement down the hall. Even when he looked away, Chris could still feel eyes on his back.

The hall ended in a small room, light gray from its carpeted floor to its high ceiling.

Despite the bitter January cold outside, the room was stuffy and hot, smelling of old coffee and stale cigarette smoke. The only light came from a bare bulb that hung well out of reach overhead. An old, battered desk and a single metal folding chair were the sole pieces of furniture. One whole wall of the room was a gleaming silver mirror. Chris suspected that it was a mirror only from inside the room. He wondered how many police officers might already be watching from the other side of the glass.

"Have a seat," said the policeman who had brought him in. He kept his hand on Chris's shoulder until Chris was settled in the cold chair.

"Now what?" Chris asked.

"Now you wait," said the policeman. "Someone will be in to talk to you in a few minutes. Okay?"

It was a long, long way from okay. Chris didn't want to be there at all, but he didn't think it would make any difference if he said that.

"Sure," he replied.

The policeman nodded. Chris watched the man's blue reflection in the mirror as he walked across the room, glanced back for a moment, then stepped out into the hallway. There was a solid click of metal as the door swung shut. Chris didn't have to try it to know that the door was locked.

Do they expect me to do something? he wondered. In the mystery novels he liked to read, the police sometimes watched a suspect when he thought he was alone. They watched him to see if he acted especially worried, or guilty. Some of the detectives in those books seemed to learn an awful lot from that kind of thing. Especially if the people being watched really were guilty.

Chris wasn't sure if he was guilty, but he was sure that he knew things he didn't want to tell the police. He decided to try his best to act normal. He sat still, with his hands folded in his lap, and stared down at the edge of the table. He forced himself to concentrate on the rough brown streaks in the gray paint of the desk, no doubt the marks left behind by previous suspects' cigarettes.

If I don't do anything, they can't learn anything, right? he thought. He glanced at the mirror. Maybe guilty people always sat still. Maybe it was innocent people who fidgeted. *Stop it. You're going to drive yourself nuts before they ask you anything.* He looked down at the worn carpet and did his best to relax.

At least the officer was telling the truth— they didn't make Chris sweat it out for more than a few minutes before the door opened and a man stepped in. He was very thin, with dull-black hair that was plastered against his skull, and a blue shadow of stubble on his narrow chin. Chris recognized him as one of the policemen who had come to the house.

Right behind him came a taller man with iron-gray hair. He had a barrel chest that strained the buttons on his uniform shirt, and massive arms that bulged under the sergeant's stripes on his sleeves. "Hello, Chris," he said.

"Mr. McAlister!" Chris said. He felt some of his tension lift. "I'm glad to see you."

The thin man snorted. "This guy a friend of yours, McAlister?" he asked.

"Friend of my daughter's," said Jake McAlister. His eyes were fixed on Chris, but he didn't offer to shake hands. The expression on his face was unreadable. "Tallibeth had him over at the house just a couple of days ago."

"Well, that's real interesting," said the other man. He leaned back against the gray wall and smiled a thin smile. "Your being friends with a fellow under investigation for murder."

"Murder!" shouted Chris. He started to stand, but Jake McAlister reached across the table and held him down.

"Don't get excited," he said. "Nobody's charging you with anything. Certainly not with murder." He shot a glance at the other man. "Watch what you say, Lansky."

The thin man gave a dry laugh. "Just trying to get a rise out of the boy."

Sergeant McAlister took his hand from Chris's shoulder and straightened. "This is

Sergeant Lansky. He's here to ask you a few questions. Just answer them as best you can." He glanced at the door with a frown. "I've got to go take care of something."

Lansky waited until the sergeant had left the room, then pulled a cigarette out of his shirt pocket. "Ready for some questions?" he sneered.

"Questions about a murder?" Chris asked. He shifted in his uncomfortable chair. "I don't know anything about a murder."

"I see," Lansky replied. "Well, then, let's talk about what you do know." He fished a cheap lighter from his pocket and rolled it around in his hand. "You knew Casey Leah Pays?"

"Casey," Chris said, trying to think fast. There had been a knot of nervousness in his stomach ever since the police had come to take him away from the house he shared with his sister. Now that knot was threatening to unravel into full-fledged panic. "I knew her," he said through a throat gone suddenly dry.

Lansky pushed himself away from the wall with a shrug of his narrow shoulders. "That's interesting. Why do you say 'knew'?"

"What?"

"You said you knew her," said Lansky. "You didn't say 'know,' you said 'knew.'" He leaned toward Chris, an expression of obviously false concern on his face. "Why do you suppose you used the past tense, Chris? Is there something

5

about Casey Pays's current condition that you know and I don't?"

Chris had seen a hundred movies and read a thousand books in which people being questioned broke down and confessed to a crime. He'd always thought it was stupid. Now that it was his turn to sit in a cold gray room and answer questions, it didn't seem so dumb.

"I said 'knew' because you said 'knew,'" he replied. "It doesn't mean anything."

Lansky nodded and lit his cigarette. "Doesn't mean a thing. Right." He stepped away from Chris and stood in the corner of the small room, puffing on his cigarette.

"Is that what this is all about?" Chris asked when the silence had stretched out for a few painful minutes. "You think I killed Casey?"

"There you go again." Lansky stepped back to the table and put his face so close to Chris that every word hit Chris's face with a blast of smoke. "Nobody said anything about Casey being dead. Why do you think she is?"

Because I put a silver knife through her chest, Chris wanted to scream out. *You see, Officer, she turned into a vampire, and I had to stab her.* For a moment the image of Casey, lying on the concrete floor and yanking at the knife, was so clear that Chris swayed in his chair.

Lansky reached out and took him by the arm. "You okay, kid? You don't look too good."

Chris nodded. "I'm all right." He pulled himself up straight in the chair and rubbed at his burning eyes. "I'd be better if you'd stop smoking."

Lansky snorted and let go of his arm. "In case you hadn't noticed, you're not in a place where you can tell other people what to do." He looked down at Chris with an expression that resembled a genuine smile. "You're not from here, are you, kid?"

Startled by the change of direction, Chris shook his head. "Chicago."

"Yeah, you sound like Chicago." Lansky dropped the cigarette on the gray carpet and ground it out under his heel. "Let me tell you something. These folks around here are a bunch of backwoods hicks. They wouldn't know a real murder if it happened in the middle of the squad room." The smile on his face turned into something else, something ugly. "But I was a real detective. NYPD, you understand?"

Chris nodded.

"If it wasn't for bloody politics, I'd still be a detective." Lansky's voice rose in pitch until he was practically screaming. "Don't you forget that! I was a real detective. This case is my chance to get out of this hick town, and you're going to help me."

He glanced at the door with its tiny window, then looked back at Chris. "I've got a dozen witnesses that say Miss Casey Pays was spending time with you. I've got her truck seen on your street the night she disappeared. I've even got someone who thinks they saw the girl going into your house." He jabbed a finger so close to Chris's nose that Chris flinched. "You tell me what happened to her, Christopher Delany from Chicago. You tell me what you did last Friday night."

Chris was afraid that the words would catch in his throat, but his voice came out with surprising strength. "On Friday I had dinner with my sister and Talli McAlister," he said. "Then Talli went home, and I went to bed."

Lansky slapped his hand down on the metal table. "You're lying to me! I don't care if you are pals with McAlister and his kid. I'll have you up on charges so fast you'll get a nosebleed. You tell me what I want to know, and you tell me now!"

A cold feeling came over Chris. He wished he had never started poking around in what had happened in Westerberg. If only he hadn't investigated the disappearances, he wouldn't have suspected that there was another vampire in town. And if he hadn't known that . . .

Then Talli would be dead, or worse, and maybe a lot of other people would be dead, too, he told himself. He had done only what he had to do.

Chris tried to pull his scattered thoughts together. He had to come up with something, some story to explain what had happened to Casey. Snippets of ideas swirled around in his skull, but he couldn't put anything together. "I—" he began.

The door to the room swung open. Both Lansky and Chris turned as a tall man with a bony face and deep-set eyes leaned through the door.

"You can't come in here right now, Mr. Pays," Lansky said.

As soon as he heard the name, Chris recognized the man as someone he had seen around the high school. He was the head football coach at the school, and Casey's father.

"Is this the one?" Coach Pays asked in a gravelly voice. "This the one that did something to my Casey?"

Lansky moved toward the man. "We're in the middle of questioning, Mr. Pays. I'm going to have to ask you to leave."

"He's the one, isn't he?" Coach Pays's blue eyes focused on Chris, and Chris could almost feel the weight of the pain churning inside the tall man. "Casey's my only child, my little girl. If you've done anything to her, I'll . . . I'll . . ." His mouth kept working, but no words came out.

Lansky stepped between the coach and Chris. "Come on, Mr. Pays. This is just questioning. You go back to my desk, and I'll talk to you in a few minutes."

The coach's eyes dulled, and he nodded. "All right," he said. Moving like a man twice his age, Casey's father shuffled out of the room.

Lansky went to close the door, but before he could, Jake McAlister stepped through. "Sorry about that," he said to Chris. "Mr. Pays came in the side door, and no one noticed him back here until they saw him through the . . . that is . . ."

"Until they saw him through the two-way mirror?" Chris asked.

The sergeant nodded. "That's right." He turned to Lansky, who was leaning against the wall. "We about finished in here?"

Lansky looked at Chris for a second, his mouth twisted in an expression of disgust. "I guess we are for now," he said. "But I'm going to talk to you again, Chris Delany, and when I do, I want some answers. Is that clear?"

Chris stood up and shoved the metal chair under the table. "I told you what I know."

"Sure you did," Lansky said. "But I think you might remember a few things you forgot to tell me."

Chris nodded quickly and headed for the door. Sergeant McAlister stepped aside to let him out.

"One more thing," Lansky called. "I think we'll want to talk to your friend, too."

"Who?" Chris asked.

"The daughter of the good sergeant here, Ms. Tallibeth McAlister," said Lansky, the unpleasant smile back on his face.

"Why do you want to talk to Talli?" her father asked.

"She was involved in the first set of disappearances back in November, and now it seems she was mixed up in this case, too." Lansky looked as if he was enjoying himself. "Yeah, I think we'll need to talk to her right away."

"Talli's got nothing to do with this," Sergeant McAlister said. He looked over at Chris, and this time his look was anything but friendly. "I don't know what this boy's told you, but if Talli knew anything about what's going on, she would have come to me."

"I'm sure she would, Sarge. I'm sure she would." Lansky leaned against the table and crossed his arms over his bony chest. "But you know, she might have seen something and not thought it was important. I definitely think she should come in."

"Talli's not feeling well," said McAlister. "You'll have to wait."

"I'll wait," Lansky said, "but not for long." He smiled again, but there wasn't a drop of warmth in his face. "I'm very eager to talk to your Talli."

He waited at the far edge of the parking lot, slouched down in the seat so no one would see him. The police didn't want him around. "It's just questioning," they had told him.

For two days now it had been "We'll keep in touch," and "You'll know as soon as we do," and "When we learn something, we'll call."

11

He didn't believe any of it. He didn't believe they'd call him, and he didn't believe they'd find Casey. Police in this town never solved anything. Thirteen kids were already missing from Westerberg, and the police hadn't found out a thing. He wasn't about to let it become fourteen.

He was ready to wait all afternoon—all night, if that's what it took—but it was only a short time before the boy came out. He watched while the boy hurried across the street and began walking down the hill away from the police station.

He lives somewhere down on the east side. Casey told me that much. He waited until the boy was almost out of sight before he started the truck and pulled out of the parking lot.

Chris Delany knew something about what had happened to Casey, and Coach Pays was determined to find out what. And he had heard the other name the police officer mentioned. If he didn't learn anything from the boy, he would see what he could get out of this Talli McAlister.

Two

❧❧❧

Talli McAlister huddled in the corner of her room, being careful to stay away from the light that leaked in around the drawn curtains.

A few more hours, and I'll be safe, she thought. She raised her hand up to her face and looked at the burn that stretched across the back and the fingers. The blisters had faded over the last two days, but the skin was still tender and red. All from ten seconds of the sun shining on her.

The light around the window turned orange, and Talli knew that the sun had reached the horizon. It was almost as if she could feel where the sun was even when she couldn't see it. In the middle of the night she still thought she could feel it burning under her feet.

Gravel crunched outside as a car pulled into

13

the drive. Talli frowned. She'd been hoping neither of her parents would get home this early. She had told them she was too sick to go to school. That was true enough. But she hadn't mentioned exactly what it was that was making her sick. It was hard enough to fake being normal when it was dark outside; it was almost impossible when the sun drove her to wrap herself in blankets and hide in the shadows.

The back door slammed, letting Talli know that her father was home. "Tallibeth!" he called from the bottom of the stairs. "You feeling any better, sweetheart?"

She opened her mouth to say no, but at that moment the sun dipped below the horizon. The itchy, uneasy feeling that had hung over her all during the day vanished as if someone had thrown a switch.

"Yes," she called to her father. "I'm feeling much better."

Talli unwrapped herself from the cocoon of blankets and walked across the wooden floor in her bare feet. The temperature outside was very low, and Talli could feel the chill of the boards underfoot in a kind of distant, distracted way. But she didn't really feel cold. She hadn't felt cold since Alex died.

When Alex had dragged her, kicking and screaming, through the snow from Chris's house to Volker's, she had felt as if she would freeze. On the way back to Chris's house, with Alex dead in the living room behind them, and the flames licking up the walls of Volker's empty house, she had felt nothing. She hadn't felt cold or heat since.

A rap on her door woke her from her memories of that night. "Can I come in?" called Mr. McAlister.

Talli glanced in the mirror. Her red hair was a tangled mess, and her skin, always pale, was white as paper. Well, at least he should believe that she had been feeling sick. "Come on in," she answered as she ran her fingers through her hair.

Her father pushed open the door and stuck his head into the room. "Nice to see you out of bed," he said. "You feel like eating something?"

Actually, Talli hadn't felt like eating in days. At her mother's insistence she had tried a piece of toast, but it had only made her feel worse. Still, she didn't want her father worrying. "Sure," she said. "I'll be right down."

"Good," said her father. "That's good." He stood in the door with an uncomfortable look on his face.

"What is it?" Talli asked.

"Howard Lansky," Mr. McAlister said. "He's been asking about Casey Pays."

"Oh." Chris had told Talli about what happened to Casey. Alex had wanted to turn Talli into a vampire, but apparently he hadn't been too sure how to do it. He'd tried it on Casey first, as an experiment, and it had worked—too well. Talli was glad she hadn't been there to see Casey's grisly end.

"He's been talking to your friend Chris," her father was saying.

"They don't think Chris has anything to do with Casey disappearing, do they?" asked Talli.

Her father shrugged his broad shoulders. "I don't know," he said. "Lansky questioned him today. I don't think it went too well." He stepped into the room and took off his uniform cap. "Listen, sweetheart, Lansky says he wants to talk to you, too."

"To me? Why would he want to talk to me?"

"You're a friend of Casey's, and of Chris's. Chris says you were together on the night Casey disappeared."

"We were," Talli said. "His sister invited me over for dinner."

Her father nodded. "I remember. That was the night of the fire over at the old Decarlo house."

Volker's house, Talli thought. The Decarlos might have lived there for years, but it would always be Volker's house as far as Talli was concerned. He had lived in the house for only a week, but Volker was the monster that had started all the killing in Westerberg, and Talli would never be able to erase her memories of what had happened in his house.

"Lansky probably just wants to talk to you

about your new friend, Chris Delany," her father continued. "He thinks Chris was involved in whatever happened to Casey."

Talli was bothered by his tone of voice. "You don't think Chris was involved, do you, Dad?"

Mr. McAlister rubbed his chin with his large, callused hand. "I don't know what to think," he said. "Did you see Casey over at the Delanys' house last Friday?"

"No," Talli said. "I didn't see Casey at all." She had been forced to lie to her parents so often lately that she was glad to give at least one true answer. Chris had told her what happened to Casey, but Talli hadn't been there to see it.

"Lansky says some people think they might have seen Casey around there. We've talked to Chris and his sister, and they've both denied seeing her." For a moment his expression was hard, but then he smiled and pushed a strand of hair away from Talli's face. "Do me a favor, sweetheart."

"What, Dad?"

"Stay away from the Delanys until this is over." Talli started to say something, but her father raised his big hands to cut her off. "I'm not saying they were involved," he told her. "I'm just saying they might have been. Lansky's going to be watching them, and I don't want him to see you together. Understand?"

"No," Talli said. "I mean, I guess I do understand why you're worried, but I've got to talk to Chris."

"You've got other friends, Talli," her father replied. "Talk to them."

"What other friends?" Talli shot back. "Lisa is gone. Alex is gone. Now Casey's gone, too. If I don't talk to Chris, just who am I supposed to talk to?"

Her father was very still for a moment; then he turned away and stared off down the hall. "You used to talk to me," he said softly.

Talli's throat tightened. Three months earlier she would have said she was closer to her father than to anyone in the world. But so many things had happened since then. "I'm sorry, Dad. I just can't."

Mr. McAlister nodded. "All right." He squared his broad shoulders. "But stay away from the Delanys."

"I can't stay away from Donna," Talli pointed out. "Not unless I don't go to school. She teaches my history class, and she's in charge of the drama club."

"Well, don't see her any more than you have to," he said firmly, "and stay away from Chris."

Talli bit her lip. She had to talk to Chris—no one else knew what was going on. Chris was the only one who might be able to do something about what was happening to her. But there was no sense fighting with her father. "Okay, I'll try," she said with a sigh. *What's one more lie when I've already told so many?* she thought.

Her father nodded. He seemed to want to say more, but he only patted her shoulder and went back downstairs.

As the light faded from around the window, Talli felt more and more restless. It was as if the house were pressing in on her—she had to get out. And there was something else, something that pressed at the back of her mind and burned in her stomach. She had hardly eaten anything since Alex had died, but tonight she felt a hunger growing. Her father's talk of dinner had stirred it up even more.

She slipped off the robe and nightshirt she had worn all day and pulled on a soft gray sweatshirt and a pair of jeans. She ran a comb through her hair until the reflection in the mirror looked vaguely presentable, then padded downstairs to find something to eat.

Her mother had come home while Talli was getting dressed. She greeted Talli with a hopeful smile. "Hi! You look like you're feeling better."

Talli nodded. "Much better." She looked past her mother at the pots simmering on the stove. "What's for supper?"

Mrs. McAlister turned to the stove and eyed the bubbling pots critically. "It's something your father started."

"Not chili again," Talli groaned.

"Nope. This time I think it's soup."

"It's beef stew," Mr. McAlister called from the pantry. He came into the kitchen with a potato in his hand. He was still dressed in his uniform, but he seemed much more relaxed. "Somebody better be careful," he said. "I almost thought I heard a complaint about my chili."

Mrs. McAlister laughed. Talli didn't join in, but she felt the tightness inside her loosen a bit. "Stew sounds good," she said. She walked over to the pot, lifted the lid, and leaned into the steam.

The smell of the stew hit her like a faceful of rotting garbage. Talli dropped the lid and staggered back from the stove, coughing.

"What's wrong?" her mother asked.

"The stew," Talli choked out. "Something must have gone bad. It smells awful."

With a puzzled look on his face, her father crossed the kitchen and looked down at the stew. "Are you sure?" he asked. "It smells fine to me."

Talli put a hand over her rolling stomach. Even from across the room the lingering smell of the stew made her feel nauseous. "Maybe it's just whatever I've got wrong with me," she said.

"I told you we should have made an appointment with the doctor," her mother said. "I'm really worried about you."

"I'll be okay, Mom," Talli said. She licked her lips and tried to smile. "Really. I guess I'm just not hungry."

"Well, don't forget you have an appointment with Dr. Aston tomorrow."

"Dr. Aston?"

Mrs. McAlister looked a bit embarrassed. "The psychiatrist, remember? You agreed to see one."

"Oh, right." Talli had forgotten all about the psychiatrist. What was she going to say to him? When her mother had first made the appointment, Talli had wondered how fast it would get her locked up if she started telling about the vampires that had been killing students in Westerberg. She didn't know, but she was willing to bet it wasn't nearly as likely to land her in a rubber room as confessing that she was turning into a vampire herself.

The nausea from the stew was fading, and hunger reasserted itself in Talli's guts. She glanced around the kitchen, but nothing there seemed like what she needed. "I think I'll go out," she said.

"You think that's a good idea?" asked her mother. "You were so sick this morning. I think you need to stay inside."

"I'll second that," added her father. "It's cold out there. No sense risking it just when you're feeling better."

"Please," Talli said. "I've been in the house for three days. I just need to get out for a few minutes."

"Well," Mrs. McAlister said slowly. "Maybe if I go with you."

21

"I'll stay in my car with the heater on," Talli said. "I won't get sick."

Her mother frowned. "Jake?"

Mr. McAlister picked up the pot lid Talli had dropped and set it down in the sink. "All right," he said, "but bundle up. I don't want you sick tomorrow morning like you have been the last three days."

Talli hurried upstairs and got her coat and car keys. As soon as she stepped out of the house, she felt better. The cold night air eased the gnawing in her gut, and the sliver of moon above seemed to light up the yard as bright as day. She savored the sharp wind against her face. She felt good. For the moment it was easy to believe that there was nothing wrong. But she knew better.

She started to get into her car, but changing her mind, she turned and walked down the driveway. Her feet crunched and squeaked over the mixture of gravel and ice. The banks of shoveled snow on either side of the drive were almost as high as Talli's chin. Along most of the driveway a line of trees screened the view, but as Talli drew near the street, she got a good look at the burned remains of Volker's house.

The fire crew had smashed down the tall privacy fence in their efforts to get near the house, but it hadn't done much good. The roof was gone, along with the siding, leaving the blackened timbers of the walls exposed to the night sky. It looked like the burned and broken rib cage of some great beast—a monstrous black skeleton on the winter ground. The snow that lay on the black timbers should have made it look clean, but it didn't—it looked like mold on a corpse. Gray ash had blown across the yard, making the snow dirty for a hundred yards in every direction.

Talli's best friend Lisa had died somewhere in the house. Alex had died there.

She had loved Alex ever since grade school. For months she'd thought he had died to feed Volker's hunger. In a way she was right. Alex had come back—or at least something that *looked* like Alex had come back. He still claimed to love Talli. He still had the same face she loved. But it hadn't been Alex, not really. The guy she loved would never have kidnapped her and taken her back to that house. It couldn't have been Alex that she'd almost killed and left to be consumed in the fire. It had been something just as evil as Volker. Talli had to believe that.

She should have been glad that the house was gone, but she wasn't. The terror that had swept Westerberg might have started in that place, but it didn't end there. Talli gripped her car keys tightly and walked back up the driveway.

The black car skidded around a curve. Gravel spun away from the rear wheels and rattled against the metal guardrail at the side of the road, sounding like the roll of a snare drum.

"You don't have to go so fast," said the girl.

The man turned to her and smiled. It was night, but he still wore dark sunglasses on his tanned, handsome face. He pushed the glasses down his nose with one finger and peered at her over the rims. "Aren't you in a hurry to get to Westerberg?" he asked.

"No," she said. She closed her eyes and shook her head. "I'm not looking forward to this."

"Why, we're only going there to help," said the man. "Westerberg should welcome us with open arms." He laughed as he steered the car around another curve.

The girl leaned away from him and rested her cheek against the cold glass of the car window. Somehow, she didn't think Westerberg would agree.

Three

"I can't take it," Donna Delany said. "All the questions. All the lies." She squeezed her dark eyes shut and shook her head frantically. "I can't do it."

Chris put his fork down on his dinner plate and looked across the table at his sister. "I don't know what to tell you," he said. "It's not easy to keep lying, but if we tell the police the truth, there's no way we'll keep them from sticking us both in a nuthouse."

Donna opened her eyes and dabbed at them with a paper napkin. "I've always known what to do, Chris," she said. "When Mom and Dad died, I knew I had to finish school and find a job. When it seemed like all our relatives wanted to break us apart, I figured out how to keep us together. But this . . .

I have no idea what to do about this."

Chris reached out and took a roll from the table as he searched for something to say. Donna was right. She was the one who always stayed calm and kept in control. No matter what happened, Chris could always count on the fact that he had the smartest and most competent—not to mention prettiest—sister in the world. It felt very strange to be trying to comfort her instead of the other way around.

"We've just got to hold tight and wait for everyone to lose interest," he said.

"How can they lose interest?" Donna asked. "Casey's dead. That's not something they're going to ignore." She tried to cut her food, but her hands were trembling so much that the knife chattered against the plate as she worked. With her short brown hair and large dark eyes, Donna had always looked younger than her age. Half the time people mistook her for a high-school student instead of a high-school teacher. Right now she looked like a frightened child.

Chris tried to sound as sure of himself as he could. "They don't know what happened to Casey," he told her. "They only know she's missing. Remember, over a dozen kids 'disappeared' from this town back in November, and they've pretty much given up on them. We've just got to go on with things, and eventually they'll give up on her, too. If we act like everything is normal, they won't be able to touch us."

Donna finished cutting her food, but made no move to eat any of it. "I wish I didn't have such a good memory," she said. "The police may not know what happened to Casey, but I do. I keep seeing her, Chris. I can't forget how she looked or what she said." A tremor ran through Donna, and she shuddered. "I can still hear her screaming."

Chris started to reply, but the doorbell sounded before he could get a word out. He pushed his chair away from the table and went to the door.

He expected it to be Sergeant Lansky. Over the last day, the police officer had brought both Chris and Donna in for questioning, and he'd called them on the phone no fewer than ten times. But when he opened the door, he saw Talli McAlister standing on the snow-covered steps.

"My father told me not to see you," she said, "but I had to come." Her red hair whipped around her face in the stiff wind. The sprinkling of freckles across her nose stood out against her pale skin.

"I need to talk to you, too," Chris said. He stepped aside to let her in.

Talli put one foot inside the door, winced, and pulled it back. "It hurts," she said.

"What?"

"When I try to come inside your house, it's like I get an electric shock." Tentatively, she

27

reached out her hand. As soon as it passed through the open door, she yanked it back. "I don't think I can come in. Maybe you can come outside with me?"

Chris tried not to show how scared he was by this new sign of what was happening to Talli. "Okay," he said. "Let me go tell Donna what's happening." He turned to find Donna already standing in the doorway to the kitchen. "I'm going out with Talli for a while," he told her.

"So I heard," his sister replied. "Can you come here for a minute? I want to talk to you."

"Go ahead," Talli said. "I'll wait."

Chris followed Donna back into the kitchen. "What's wrong?"

"You can't go with her," Donna answered in a fierce whisper.

"Why not?" he asked.

"Why not? Because you told me yourself that she's one of those . . . those . . . *things* now. The things that almost killed us both! The same thing Casey turned into! That's why not!" She looked over Chris's shoulder as she spoke, as if nervous that Talli might come charging in.

"I didn't say that," Chris protested.

"No, you just said that her skin burns to a crisp every time the sun hits it," Donna hissed back. "And I heard her say it hurts to try and come in our house. Come on, Chris. She's not just some girl from down the street; she's a vampire. You can't go out there in the dark with her."

"Talli's not a vampire. Just look at her. You remember how Alex and Casey acted." Chris jerked his thumb at the front door, where Talli still stood outside in the snow. "Do you see Talli acting like they did?"

"No, but . . ." Some of the fire and fear went out of Donna's eyes. "No, I guess she isn't. But she scares me, Chris. I like Talli, but I don't want anything to happen to you." She gave him a tight hug. "You're my family. You're all I've got."

"I'll be careful," Chris said. "But I have to see if there's some way I can help Talli."

Donna nodded and let him go. "Don't stay out too late," she said. "Remember, it's a school night."

Chris choked back laughter. School seemed so trivial compared to what had gone on since he had arrived in Westerberg. Everyday life was something that happened only to other people. "We'll get back as soon as we can," he replied.

He pulled his heavy jacket off the coat rack and walked back into the living room. Talli was still on the porch, her face turned to the cold dark night. She spun around as Chris came out the door.

"I can see," she said. She seemed surprised about it.

Chris frowned. "That's good. So can I."

Talli shook her head. "No, I mean I can see in the dark." She turned back to the night and

29

pointed across the windswept street. "It just started a few minutes ago, but everything is getting clearer all the time. There's a cat over there in the shadows. I can see it trying to get into some garbage cans. Down at the end of the street someone dropped a mitten in the snow."

"I don't see anything," Chris said, craning his neck to look past Talli.

"I do. I can see it as clear as day."

Chris tried to read the expression on her face. He wanted to see horror there, wanted Talli to be upset about what was happening. *He* was terrified, and it bothered him that Talli seemed so calm. He reached back and closed the door. "Come on, let's get out of here before I freeze."

Talli nodded and walked down the steps to her car. "That's another thing," she said as she got in. "Did I tell you? I don't feel cold at all."

"Yeah, well, I do." Chris jumped into the car and rubbed his hands together. "Let's get moving."

Talli steered up the street past the scorched wreck of Volker's house. She didn't say anything more about her new abilities, and Chris didn't know what to say, so they drove in silence through downtown Westerberg. They passed the empty school, then a cluster of houses, and then they were out among the woods and fields of the countryside. Chris looked out the window and saw nothing but the light of a distant farmhouse.

The winter woods were as dense and dark as spilled ink.

"Can you really see out there?" he asked finally.

"Everything. It's different, though. It's like I'm not seeing with my eyes, but with some other part of me. Everything is a shade of brown or red, like one of those really old photos where everything's a strange color. But it's sharp, and there's more . . . I don't know . . . depth, maybe. I can't describe it."

"And this just started?" Chris asked.

"Like I said, it started tonight. As soon as it began to get dark, I felt really restless. But when I went outside, at first I thought it was still light. Then I realized it was dark, but I could still see."

Chris looked at her dim profile as she steered the car down the country road. He had hoped that the strange things happening to Talli would get better with time, but instead they were getting worse. And worst of all was the way she was talking about it. "You don't seem too upset," he said. "Doesn't this bother you?"

"I don't know how I should feel," Talli said. "In the daytime, when the sun is burning me, it seems like the end of the world. But when the night rolls around, I feel . . ." She shrugged. "Like I said, I don't know how I feel."

Suddenly she slammed on the brakes. The car skewed to the side, straightened, then skidded over icy patches on the road and began to

31

turn around and around. Chris dug his fingers into the seat as the car spun. It was traveling tail-first when it smacked into a wall of hard-packed snow thrown up by a passing plow. The impact brought Chris's head down against the dashboard with a force that sent stars whirling across his vision.

"What are you doing?" he shouted as he bounced back against his seat.

Talli sat bolt upright. "Look over there," she said. "See it?" She pointed out the window, past the mounds of snow and into the dark trunks of the forest that lined the road.

Chris leaned past her, rubbing his head. The lights from the car carved yellow paths through the night, making the snow sparkle, but the woods were so dense that they seemed to swallow the light. No matter how he squinted, Chris couldn't see anything in the dark but dark. "What am I looking for?" he asked.

Instead of answering Talli opened her door and stepped outside. "Talli?" Chris called. "What do you think you're doing?"

"I've got to see what it is," she replied. "I've never seen anything like it." Leaving her car door hanging open, she walked across the street, hesitated for a moment at the edge of the road, then jumped over the snowbank and vanished into the dark woods.

"Talli!" Chris called. "Talli, come back!" He pushed open his door and climbed out.

Immediately his feet slipped in the snow, and he sat down hard on the edge of the road. "Great," he said. "This is really wonderful."

He held on to the side of the car as he got to his feet. Carefully, he shut his door and shuffled around the car. He reached inside, pulled out the keys, and punched off the lights. With the headlights gone there was no light but the cold moon overhead. Chris slammed Talli's door shut. Then he walked across the street and squinted into the darkness. "Talli!" he called again. He thought he heard a faint reply, but he couldn't be sure. *Well*, he thought. *Do I wait, or do I follow?* With a groan Chris trudged off the road and into the snow.

Talli had leaped the plowed-up snowbank, but Chris fell two more times before he got over it. Crouching in order to see the ground, he followed the line of Talli's footprints toward the black tree trunks.

The moon was skittering between rapidly moving clouds, casting silver shadows across the snow on the road. But as soon as Chris entered the woods, it was as dark and close as the inside of a cave. He had to stop several times and get down on his hands and knees to see Talli's footprints. In less than a dozen steps Chris could no longer see the road. By the time he had gone a hundred yards, he was soaking wet and half-frozen.

There was still no sign of Talli when Chris

33

realized that the footprints he was following were his own. He backed up, trying to find where he had gone wrong. He came to a place he remembered passing before, where the broken stump of a twisted cedar tree jutted up from the snow. He started following the footsteps again, until he came back to the same place. He was lost. Panic seized Chris—he didn't know whether to run or stand still. Something moved at the corner of his eye. He whirled around.

"Talli?" he said, but it was barely a whisper. If something really had moved, it wasn't moving now.

At least it seemed a little brighter in that direction. With fear still holding on to his heart, Chris walked away from the stump. Almost at once he came into a clearing where the moon shone down and weeds stuck out of the snow. Twenty feet away Talli McAlister stood beside a mass of gray stone, staring down at the ground. There was something about the way she was standing that kept Chris's heart beating double time.

"Talli?" he said softly. "Are you okay? What are we doing here?"

She turned to him, a blank expression on her face. "It's a cemetery," she said. "That's what I was seeing back in the car, a cemetery."

Until she said the word, Chris hadn't realized that the stone beside her was the weathered remains of a small crypt. There were other vaults on the far edge of the clearing, and the rounded tops of old tombstones leaned from the snow like rotting teeth.

"Can you see it?" Talli asked.

"I can see the stones," Chris said.

She shook her head. "Not the stones, the light." She waved her hands around her. "There's a glow around this whole place."

Chris shook his head. "No. I can't see anything."

"Well, I can see it," Talli said, glancing back at the weathered tomb. "It's like green fire that burns right through the snow." She put a hand on the cracked top of the decaying crypt. "It's kind of like the light I see around people, but not quite."

Chris could feel the hairs at the back of his neck rising. "You see a light around people?"

She nodded. "I can see it around you right now, Chris."

Suddenly the dark woods seemed more inviting to Chris than this moonlit place. "Come on, Talli," he said. "Let's get out of here."

She turned back to him, and even in the dim light of the moon, he could see that tears were coursing down her pale cheeks. Through the deaths of Alex and Casey, and all the terrible things that had happened, Chris couldn't remember ever seeing Talli cry. Just minutes before, he had wanted her to be more upset, but now that she was, it didn't make Chris feel any better.

"I'm scared, Chris," she said. "It's like the light was talking to me and I had to come. It wants me to do something. I just couldn't stop myself. What if I get like that with people? What might I do to them? What might I do to you?" She looked up at the night sky. "I think you should get away from me now, before I do something."

Chris waded through the knee-deep snow to reach her. "I'm not going anywhere," he said. "I'm staying with you until we find a way to get rid of this thing."

She reached out and took his hand. Though she was trembling, her fingers held his with enough strength to make him wince.

"Careful," he said. "I'm here, but I'm fragile."

A laugh escaped her, but it didn't lessen the worry on her face. She looked at him with tear-bright eyes. Then she leaned forward and kissed him. "I don't want to be like Volker," she whispered, her lips still close to Chris's face. "Don't let me be a monster."

"I won't. I don't know what to do," he said, "but I promise I'll find out."

"I believe I might be of some assistance there," said a voice.

His hands still linked with Talli's, Chris twisted around to see a slim man in a long trench coat step from the shadows under the trees. Despite the calm expression on the man's face, there was something menacing about him as he advanced toward them.

"Stay back," Chris shouted.

"If I stay back," said the stranger, "then how can I help?" Moonlight played along his teeth as his lips parted in a wide smile. Behind him, Chris saw another figure moving through the shadows.

"Who are you?" Chris asked. He started to step forward, but Talli pulled him back.

"No, Chris, don't. It's Them."

"It's who?" asked Chris.

"I believe she means we are vampires," said the smiling man. "And she's quite right."

Four

Talli put her hand on Chris's shoulder and stepped in front of him. "What do you want?" she called.

The vampire leaned over and brushed the snow from the top of a lichen-stained tombstone, then sat down on it. The tail of his coat hung nearly to his feet, grazing the snow. In Talli's vision the vampire was cloaked in a swirling glow that pulsated and danced with color. Tendrils of green light reached up from the ground to follow his every movement.

"We came here looking for someone," he said. "I thought it was you, but now I can see I'm mistaken."

"You were looking for Volker, weren't you?" Talli asked. "You came to help him."

The vampire leaned back and shoved his

hands into the pockets of his long trench coat. His face was very narrow and angular, his eyes a smoky gray. Talli thought he looked to be about twenty-five, but she knew from her experiences with Volker and Alex that vampires could look however they wanted.

"Volker," he said. "Is that the name of the one who is here?" His voice was smooth and calm, with a trace of an accent—maybe British, maybe not.

Chris leaned in to whisper in Talli's ear. "When I say 'go,' we run for the woods. If we get to the trees, we can lose them."

Talli shook her head. "No," she whispered back. "I can see fine, even in the woods. He can probably see even better."

"And I hear very well," said the vampire, "and run very, very fast. Please, let's not end this conversation until we've exchanged some meaningful information."

The other vampire stepped out of the trees. She was tall, with a shaggy cap of dark hair, and eyes that were jet-black even in Talli's strange new vision. She was very thin, and her movements were loose and almost clumsy. She looked to be no older than Chris and Talli.

"Ah, you've decided to join us," said the male vampire. "Come over here and sit with me." He patted the cold tombstone with his long, thin hand. The girl hesitated for just a moment, then walked over to the man, but she didn't sit down.

"This is Sky," he said. "And my name is Seth."

Talli didn't introduce herself or Chris. "You said you were looking for someone," she said. "Who?"

"If this Volker is the one that made you, then I suppose it's him I'm after." He smiled again. "But not, I expect, for the reasons you might think." He reached out and put an arm around Sky's waist, pulling her close. "You see, we're here to clean up."

"Clean up?" Talli asked. "Clean up what?"

"It's come to our attention that something has been going on in your town," said Seth. "From the description I've heard, it seems that we have a renegade vampire on the loose."

Chris stepped up to Talli's side. "Who told you?" he asked.

"I read it in the papers," said Seth.

"No." Chris shook his head. "You can't read every paper in the world, and even if you did, no paper has written the truth about this town. So who told you Volker was a vampire?"

"Come now," Seth said. "Almost two dozen unexplained deaths and disappearances in a town this small over such a short period? There are not so many of us as to catch everything right away, but when someone acts up as badly as this Volker, they are hard to miss."

Chris took a half step forward. "A second ago you called Volker a renegade, and now you say

41

he was acting badly. Do you mean that vampires aren't supposed to kill people?"

"Of course not," said Seth. "Why should we? We can maintain ourselves quite well by sipping only a tiny bit of energy from those around us. A gold who takes to killing greens can cause quite a bit of trouble for the rest of us."

"Golds and greens?" Talli asked.

"I'm sorry," Seth replied. "Those words mean nothing to you, do they? You see, we tend to regard 'vampire' as something of a derogatory term. We call normal people greens because they are usually surrounded by a green light when we see them at night. We call ourselves golds because . . ." He stopped and gave another of his wide smiles. "I suppose we call ourselves golds because we tend to be quite vain."

Talli almost found herself smiling with him. His soothing voice and charming words were draining away her fear.

"So you came here to stop Volker," Chris said. "To clean up Westerberg."

Seth nodded. "That's right. We have to keep him from drawing the attention of the green authorities." He pulled his arm from behind Sky and clapped his hands together. "So where is this Volker?"

"It's too late," Talli started. "I—"

Chris suddenly grabbed her arm. "Volker's gone," he said. "We don't know where."

Talli stared at him. Chris knew perfectly well

what had happened to Volker. Why would he lie?

Seth's smiled faded. "That's a real shame," he said. "Still, I suppose this town is glad to see him go. Perhaps we can find some clues that will help us learn your Mr. Volker's next stop."

"You'll be leaving Westerberg, I guess?" Chris asked.

"As soon as we're sure Volker is really gone," Seth said. "I trust we can count on you to provide us with any information you can?" He stood up and dusted the snow from his jacket.

"Sure," Talli said, still looking at Chris. "I don't see why not."

"There is one other thing we must take care of," Seth said. "And that is you."

Talli forced herself not to move as he walked slowly though the snow and stopped just a step away from her.

"Can you fix me?" she asked nervously.

"Fix? Ah, you mean make you back into a green. Back into what you think of as a normal person." He shrugged. "I don't know. How did it happen that you should be half one thing and half another?"

Talli started to answer, but Chris leaned in and spoke quickly. "The police came in. Volker had to run."

Seth's gray eyes turned to Chris. "Really?" For just a moment Seth's angular face looked as hard and cold as a marble statue; then he turned

43

back to Talli. "However this occurred, it must be very uncomfortable for you."

"Yes," Talli agreed quickly. She was glad he was talking to her instead of pressing Chris for more details. Everything Chris had said to Seth was a lie, and Talli had a terrible feeling that Seth knew it.

"I'm afraid you are too far from human to be comfortable in the sunlight," Seth said, "but not far enough along to feed. Without help you will slowly lose energy. Eventually, you'll have none left."

"Does that mean I'll die?"

"Yes," Seth said, "but not quickly, and not without quite a bit of pain."

"We can't let that happen," Chris said firmly.

Seth's expressive face showed great concern. "No, of course not." He touched the tips of his long fingers to Talli's chin and lifted it so that the moonlight fell across her face. "I cannot make you back into a green," he said, "but I can help you."

Talli stood very still, enjoying the electric sensation of Seth's touch. It felt as if all the nerves in her body had suddenly moved to her chin. She could feel every detail of his fingers, right down to each groove of his fingerprint. "What can you do?" she asked.

"I can give you some of my energy," Seth said.

Memories of her last minutes with Alex

came swirling up in Talli's mind. She had felt him pulling her down into nothing, draining the spark of life from her body. Then energy had come flooding back into her in a burning torrent. That was how she had gotten to this halfway state. If Chris hadn't interrupted them, Alex would have given her enough energy to make her a full vampire.

"If I take some of your energy," she asked Seth, "won't that make me more a vampire?"

Seth smiled again. "No. It could, but the way I'll do it now shouldn't change you. What it will do is allow you to face the day without pain. I assume you have been pretending to be a green?"

"Yes," she said, "but it's been hard when I spend the day hiding in the shadows."

He lowered his hand from her face. "This will make it easier," he replied. "You will be able to go on with your normal life tomorrow, while I try to think of a more permanent solution."

"Maybe we should think about it," Chris suggested. "You don't want to make any snap decisions, Talli."

But Talli couldn't drag her eyes away from Seth. His eyes remained fixed on Talli's face. "Your friend doesn't trust me," he said. "I suppose if he has had experience with a renegade, then he has good reason to be afraid. But I am not here to hurt you. Please believe that."

He raised his hands with the palms turned

toward Talli and Chris. "Please, my kind has already caused so much trouble in this small town, let me do this one thing to help."

Talli hesitated. Volker had been capable of sounding perfectly reasonable. Half the people in town had thought he was a great guy. Talli had known better, but did that mean her judgment would always be good? Maybe Seth really wanted to help.

It was the thought of what would happen if she didn't take Seth's energy that finally helped her decide. She wouldn't be able to stand another day wrapped in blankets while the sun waited to fry her. "Let's try it," she said.

"Talli," Chris said uneasily, "are you sure?"

Talli nodded, but didn't trust herself to say anything more.

Seth reached out again and lightly rested his fingers on her face. For a moment Talli felt the same electric sensation she had felt on his first touch. Then liquid fire poured from his hands. Talli threw back her head and squeezed her eyes shut as energy seared through her, coursing down every nerve and through every muscle. She felt it in her feet and her hands. She felt it blaze through her bone, and dance along her teeth. Then Talli was falling.

She felt Chris's hands under her and heard a mumble of voices. "I'm okay," she said.

She opened her eyes and gasped. She had thought her night vision was as good as it could get, but she had been wrong. Every bare winter branch, every dry brown weed, every time-worn stone, glinted with an inner light. The vampires, Seth and Sky, were whirls of rainbow. Chris was a blaze of emerald fire as he helped her sit up in the snow.

"Everything's different," she said. "It's as bright as noon."

"I should have warned you," Seth said. "Be careful getting back to your car. Seeing like this can be a bit distracting at first."

"Are you ready to go?" Chris asked.

"Am I?" Talli asked Seth.

"For now," he replied. "But remember, while exposure to sunlight won't hurt you at first, it will drain your energy. If you stay in the sun too long, then it will begin to cause pain. In any case, you will need to meet me again tomorrow night so I can provide the additional energy you'll need."

"Or tell us how to get her back to normal," Chris said.

"Of course," Seth said with a smile. He turned to his silent companion. "Come, Sky. Let's leave these two alone."

"Wait," Talli said. "How will we find you tomorrow night?"

Seth turned back and flashed another grin. "Don't worry. We'll find you." Then he and Sky entered the woods. For a few seconds after they had passed out of sight, Talli could still see the

47

smudge of multicolored light that marked their trail.

"Are you sure you're all right?" Chris asked.

Talli nodded. "I think so. I feel better than I did. In fact, I feel better than I *ever* did."

Chris frowned. "I don't like the sound of that."

"You don't want me to feel good?" Talli asked.

"No," he said. "I don't want you to feel good right after getting energy from a vampire. It scares me, Talli, and it should scare you, too."

He turned away from her and trudged away through the snow. Following behind him, it was all Talli could do to keep herself from running. She felt so strong and fast, she was sure she could fly over the snow if she tried.

"Why didn't you let me say anything about Alex?" she asked as Chris picked his way back through the black trunks.

"I didn't want to tell them everything," he said. "We don't really know why they're here."

Talli stopped and looked at Chris in surprise. "They're here to find Volker," she said. "You heard that. And Seth can help me, Chris. If we lie to him, we might ruin things."

"How do you know he can help?" Chris asked.

"He's already helped. I'll be able to go to school tomorrow instead of hiding like a bat in a cave."

Chris turned around and looked at her in the darkness. Talli could tell by the way he was squinting that he saw nothing of her but a dim silhouette. She could see every detail of his face. His brown eyes were filled with worry.

"How do you know the energy he gave you didn't push you closer to being a vampire?" he asked.

"Because . . ." Talli's voice trailed off. A moment ago she had been confident. It had all felt so good.

"You know because Seth told you, right?" Chris said.

"I guess so," Talli said, "but I think we can trust him."

"I don't. Vampires can look like anyone, and they can sound like anyone. I think Seth put on a great act, but I don't believe a bit of it."

He turned and began to push onward through the woods, leaving Talli alone in the snow. The cold didn't affect her, but she felt a chill anyway. *What if Chris is right?* she thought. *Have I made things worse?*

"Chris," she called, moving easily through the trees to catch up with him. "What about the other lie? Why didn't you tell Seth what happened to Volker? Now he's going to spend a lot of time looking for someone who's dead."

"I hope so," Chris said.

"But why?"

"Seth said that vampires take care of other

49

vampires that kill humans," he replied. "I don't know if that's true, but I do know one thing." He pushed through a group of thin trees and came out into the moonlight near the side of the road. In the silver light he turned to face Talli.

"I'll bet you anything they take care of humans that kill vampires."

Coach Pays focused the binoculars. It was getting cold in the truck, and the windows were fogging over. If the two he was after didn't come out of the woods soon, he'd have to crank up the engine and turn on the heat for a while. He didn't want to do that.

The truck was hidden amid the rusted hulks of some old tractors about a half mile from where the McAlister girl had parked her orange car. He didn't think anyone would notice his battered pickup just by looking. But if he started the engine, they might hear it.

Figures moved along the tree line. Coach Pays ran his hand along the damp windshield and stared through the binoculars. It was the other two he had seen go into the woods—the man in the coat and the dark-haired girl. Coach Pays wasn't sure if these two had anything to do with what had happened to Casey, but he suspected they did. Otherwise, they wouldn't be meeting with the Delany boy out in the middle of nowhere. He noted the license number of their black car on a scrap of paper.

Could be there was a drug deal involved, he thought. *Maybe my Casey found out this Delany was in with drug dealers and tried to stop him.* He didn't follow up on that thought. Most ideas he came up with ended with Casey's being dead, and that was something he wasn't ready to think about.

The black car pulled away. For long minutes there was no sign of the two he'd been following. He started to wonder if maybe a deal had gone bad. Maybe this time it was Delany and the girl who would turn up missing. He was even thinking about driving down for a closer look, when the two emerged from the woods.

The Delany boy struggled and fell getting over the snow. The McAlister girl danced over it. *Good athlete,* thought Coach Pays. *Of course, not as good as my Casey.* The lights came on in the orange car, and it began to pull away.

Coach Pays put down his binoculars and followed.

Five

Tuesday

"You really think Talli is feeling better?" Donna asked.

Chris swallowed a bite of cereal and nodded. "Yeah," he said. "Much better."

Donna's brown eyes narrowed into slits. "I'm not so messed up that I can't tell when you're lying to me," she said.

"No, really. I think she'll be at school today," he said. *It's tonight that worries me,* he thought. *No matter what Talli thinks, I don't trust Seth.*

Donna didn't look convinced. "I guess I'll see her in class." She stood up and smoothed down her tan skirt. "You'd better ride in with me—there's too much snow on the sidewalks to walk."

"Sounds good to me." Chris downed the last of his milk, then raced upstairs to get his things. When he got back to the kitchen, Donna was pushing things around on the counter and opening and closing drawers.

"All right," she said. "Where did you hide the car keys this time?"

Chris smiled. "I hid them right where you left them. They're on top of the radio."

Donna grabbed the keys and headed for the door. "Come on," she said. "I don't want to be late."

Chris held on to the railing as he went down the slippery steps, crunched across the driveway, and hopped into the cold car. Swirls of white fell away as the wipers pushed aside the light dusting of snow that had fallen overnight.

He looked at the ruins of Volker's burned-out house as they drove past. Unlike Talli, Chris had never met Volker. His only experience with vampires was from his meeting with Alex Cole, who had been Talli's boyfriend before Volker had turned him into a monster.

Chris closed his eyes, trying to remember anything that might help. Alex had been cruel, strong, and powerful. But he hadn't been too smart. He had acted confused, and his attempts to win Talli over to his side hadn't been very sophisticated. Seth didn't seem to be like Alex. He appeared to be in control of himself. He was slick, Chris gave him that much, but it didn't make him any less a monster. In Chris's book it only made him a more dangerous monster.

They reached downtown Westerberg, and Chris opened his eyes to look out at Main Street. The major snowstorm had happened almost a week before, and the town was beginning to lose the picture-book prettiness it had when the snow was fresh. Gray slush lay in the gutters along the sides of the road. Sidewalks in front of the open stores were scraped clean and sprinkled with coarse salt. In other places the sidewalk was still covered in snow broken by only a few footprints. These white stretches marked the stores that were no longer in business. In the week since Chris and Donna had moved to town, two stores had closed. All the disappearances and deaths that had started months before were draining the life out of Westerberg just as surely as Volker had drained the life from his victims.

When they reached the school, there were no more than a dozen cars in the parking lot. Donna headed for the teachers' lounge, and Chris took a seat in his first-period room. He pulled a book out of his backpack and tried to get interested in math homework. After five minutes he slammed the book closed.

He couldn't concentrate enough to work on algebra when his mind was full of thoughts of Talli and what might happen to her. He thought if he could have met Volker and seen what he was like, he might have felt better about Seth. Talli had met Volker, and Talli seemed to trust Seth. Did that mean that Seth was okay, or was it just that Talli wasn't thinking straight? A headache began to form behind Chris's eyes. He sorted through his books, pulled out his history text, and tried his best to lose himself in the events of the civil rights movement until the room filled with students and the school day began.

As Chris was pushing his tray along the metal rails in the lunch line, a hand settled on his arm. "Hi," Talli said brightly.

"Hi." Chris looked at the smile on her face and the shine in her green eyes. "You look like you're feeling good."

She nodded. "I am. Seth—" She stopped and lowered her voice. "Seth was right. Whenever I get in the sunlight, I start feeling kind of draggy. But it doesn't burn, and as soon as I get back in the shade, I feel great."

"Are you going to eat anything?" Chris asked. "It doesn't look too bad today."

"I don't think so," Talli said. She shrugged. "I don't feel hungry."

"I think you should eat something," Chris said. "You have enough problems—you shouldn't starve on top of it."

Talli leaned past him and looked at the food behind the glass of the counter. Her nose wrinkled up in disgust. "I don't think so," she said. "Maybe later."

She waited while Chris paid for his food. They walked away from the register, and Chris craned his neck looking for an open table in the crowded room.

"We could go outside and eat," Talli suggested.

"It's twenty degrees outside," Chris said. "Maybe you don't get cold anymore, but I sure do." He finally located a table in a remote corner, and they settled in as far from anyone else as they could get.

Chris noticed a few of the other students looking at them and whispering. Whenever anyone saw that he was looking back, they turned away quickly. He wondered how much of it was social gossip—the new kid in town and all that—and how much of it had to do with what had been going on in Westerberg. He certainly wouldn't put it past Officer Lansky to start a few rumors just to make things a bit hotter.

"When do you want to get together tonight?" Talli asked.

"I don't know." Chris looked around to make sure no one was listening. "Do we really have to meet Seth?" he asked.

"You heard what he said," Talli replied. "He only gave me enough energy to last through a day. If I don't get more tonight, I'll be back to hiding from the sun." She shook her head. "I can't take that."

Chris reached across the table and took her hand. "I'm still not convinced that he's really trying to help you."

Talli's small mouth turned down in a frown. "I guess I'm not either, not completely. But he did help me last night. Besides, what else can I do?"

Chris wished he had a good answer for that. "I'm going back to the library today," he said. "I know that these monsters aren't really like the vampires in the old books, but maybe we can find some way to turn you back."

"Turn me back," Talli repeated. "It sounds so weird. Like I'm not me anymore."

"You're still you," Chris said. "I just want to make sure it stays that way." He glanced up at the clock on the cafeteria wall. Lunch was half over, and he still hadn't touched his food. "Can you give me a lift to the library after school?" he asked. "I'd walk, but the roads are a mess out there."

"I can't," said Talli. She leaned across the table and spoke in a whisper. "There's a drama-club meeting after school, and then I'm supposed to go see a psychiatrist. My parents made the appointment for me."

Chris sat back in his chair, his mouth open in surprise. "What are you going to tell him?"

Talli shrugged. "I don't know. I guess I'm going to say as little as I can get away with. I'll try to call you as soon as I get back. That is, I will if my dad's not looking."

"Okay." Chris glanced again at the wall clock. "I'll go see if I can use Donna's car while she's handling drama club." He stood and picked up his tray. "I better run if I'm going to talk to her before lunch is over."

"You didn't eat anything," Talli said with a nod toward his tray.

Chris looked down at the food on his plate. "You know, for some reason I'm not feeling too hungry myself."

He left the lunchroom and walked down the long hall to the classroom where Donna taught. "Donna, can I—" he started as he stepped through the door. Then he saw that a man was standing in front of his sister's desk. "I'm sorry," he said. "I didn't mean to interrupt."

The man turned and looked at Chris with dark-blue eyes set deep in a bony face. "Come on in," Coach Pays said. "We were just talking about my Casey."

Chris swallowed and stepped hesitantly into the room. "I'm really sorry that Casey is missing," he said. "She was very nice to me."

Coach Pays gave a bitter laugh. "She was nice to you, and look where it got her!"

Donna spoke out from the other side of Coach Pays. "I've been trying to tell him we don't know what happened to Casey," she said, "but he thought we might be able to remember something we didn't tell the police."

The coach took a step toward Chris. "I've

heard that happens sometimes," he said. "You forget things when you're sitting up there at the police station, but you remember them later."

He came over and stood just in front of Chris. He was very tall—Chris's eyes were not even at the level of Pays's sharp chin. The tendons stood out in his thin neck, and a muscle twitched at the corner of his clenched jaw. His plain white shirt smelled like old sweat.

"Casey was running around with you nearly every day last week," he continued. "I would have thought you knew where she went."

Fighting off the desire to step away, Chris looked up into Pays's narrow face. "If I remember anything," he said, "I'll be sure to tell you."

The coach snorted. His thin lips twisted back in disgust, and for a moment Chris was sure the man was going to hit him. "You do that," he said at last. "My Casey would never have run off on her own. Somebody knows where she is, and I'm going to find out." He stepped around Chris and stomped quickly out of the room.

"He knows," Donna said as Chris walked up to her desk. "He knows we had something to do with Casey disappearing."

Chris shook his head. "I don't think so. He was down at the police station when I came in. He's probably just talking to us because Lansky did."

Donna sat down in her chair and put her hands over her face. "What are we going to do?"

she said. "Someone is going to find out, and then we'll both be charged with murder."

"We didn't kill Casey," Chris said firmly. "Alex Cole did that. The thing I stabbed wasn't Casey. It was a monster that Alex made."

Donna slid her fingers aside and looked up at him. "Like Talli, Chris? If Casey was a monster you had to kill, what does that make Talli?"

"Talli's not a monster."

"Not yet," Donna said.

"Maybe not ever," Chris answered. "Listen, I just came in to ask for the car while you're doing the drama club. I want to go up to the library and see what I can find that might help. If it looks like there might be something there, maybe we can both go back after the drama-club meeting and work on it."

"I guess so," said his sister. "I've got nothing else to do but go home and worry."

"Don't worry so much," Chris said. "We've only done what we had to, and there's no way anyone can prove we had anything to do with Casey."

Donna managed a small smile. "Oh, let me worry. I do it so well."

Afternoon classes seemed to take about six hours each. In math Chris gave up on listening to the teacher and concentrated on what he might do to help Talli. He wished he had paid more attention to horror movies and books. Talli liked that stuff, but detective stories and

61

British mysteries were more to Chris's taste.

He flipped open his notebook. At the top of a blank page he wrote "Volker." He circled the name, then drew a line down the page. In another circle, he wrote "Alex," and in circles below that, "Casey" and "Talli."

In a lot of ways vampirism seemed like a disease. It spread from one person to another, with each vampire acting as a carrier that could make other vampires. Thinking of it as a disease, Chris wrote down the things he knew about the symptoms:

Vampires are sensitive to light.

Sunlight burned Talli, and she'd told him that several of Volker's newly made vampires had died when she had exposed them to the sun. Seth had warned that too much sunlight could hurt Talli even after he had given her some of his energy. *If Talli is really half-vampire and half-normal,* Chris thought, *would exposure to sunlight really kill her? Maybe it would only kill the vampire part and leave the human part alive.*

He wrote the idea down on his pad, but he was in no hurry to try it. If it didn't work, Talli could die. Even if it did work, it seemed sure to be very painful.

Vampires don't like silver.

Both Chris and Talli had seen vampires take terrible blows from ordinary weapons without much damage. But a small silver corkscrew had been enough for Talli to kill Volker, and a silver knife had done in Casey. Chris knew that silver was a very good conductor. Maybe it did something to the energy that the vampires seemed to live on. Would copper work as well? If he wrapped Talli in silver wire, could it somehow drain off the vampire energy without hurting her? Chris knew he was clutching at straws, but he wrote down the idea anyway.

Vampires can be killed by fire.

Fire had killed Alex after they had wounded him so badly that he couldn't escape the burning house. That didn't seem to offer any cures for Talli. Throwing her in a fire to make her normal seemed like a pretty bad idea.

When the bell sounded at the end of the day, Chris put the rest of his books in his locker, but kept the notebook to take with him to the library. He started for Donna's car, but a familiar figure was waiting for him in the hallway.

"Good afternoon, Mr. Delany," said Sergeant Lansky. "I think we need to talk." Lansky seemed almost happy.

He's found something, Chris thought. The police could have gotten a warrant and gone into the house while he and Donna were at school. Casey's body had crumbled into dust when she was destroyed, and they had burned her clothing until there was next to nothing left, but in some of Chris's detective books, that was all it took.

"I've already told you everything I know," he said.

63

Lansky nodded. "I'm sure you have. Thing is, I had a talk with the Chicago police. Seems that your parents died just a few months ago."

"They didn't *die*," Chris said. "Someone killed them."

"That's exactly what the Chicago PD told me," Lansky said. "And you know what else they said? They said they never found out who did it."

For a moment Chris had no idea why Lansky was bringing this up. Then the blood began to hammer in his ears, and his hands tightened into fists. "You're telling me you think I had something to do with my parents' murder?"

Lansky pulled a crumpled pack from his pocket, knocked out a cigarette, and put it between his nicotine-yellowed teeth. "Let's go down to the station and talk about it," he said.

Six

❧❧❧

Many times in the past Talli had been frightened to go into the school auditorium. She had first met Volker in the dimly lit hallway behind the stage. Later Volker had created some kind of ghostly monster that chased her through the dark rows of seats on the night that her best friend, Lisa, had disappeared. Ever since, the auditorium had been a reminder of all the terrible things that had happened.

This time it was different. During two of Talli's afternoon classes, the winter sun had slanted in through the windows. The windows were tall, and no matter where Talli sat, the sunlight was always on her. At first the sunlight had caused no more than a tickling sensation. But by the end of the last period, Talli was starting to feel very uncomfortable. Getting into the dim shadows of the auditorium, where there were no windows to let in the burning sun, felt great.

About thirty students were already grouped in the first three rows in front of the stage. Talli sat down and listened to them talking excitedly about the upcoming play. For several years the drama club had done only one or two plays a season. It always seemed to be the same play every year, and it had gotten to the point where even the parents hated to come. But Ms. Delany had put the club on a tough schedule, with three new plays planned before the end of the year.

The first was coming up in just a few weeks, and people were scrambling to learn their lines, build scenery, make posters, and take care of all the hundreds of things involved in staging a production. Ms. Delany had brought a lot of new kids into the club, and now the "regulars" were having to act as teachers, showing the newcomers how things were done backstage. Talli had done scenery in the past, and she talked with a few of the other students about the next production. Fortunately, it was a play with very simple staging, and nothing more than backgrounds needed to be made.

Watching Grant Winchell boss the student actors around was one of the most entertaining things Talli had done in a long time. Grant had always been the kind of guy who was so quiet, he disappeared into the woodwork. Since Ms.

Delany had picked him to be director for the up-coming play, Grant had really come out of his shell. He was running from one group to another, jumping in and out of conversations, and clearly having the time of his life.

Talli watched Ms. Delany walk down the aisle and take her place at the foot of the stage. She seemed tense. Usually she walked back and forth, lighting up the room with her enthusiasm. Today she seemed kind of flat. It was easy enough for Talli to guess why, especially since Ms. Delany kept glancing up at her, then looking away.

After the group had discussed the upcoming play, Talli went down to the front to talk to Ms. Delany. "I know I'm supposed to help plan the scenery," she said, "but I've got to leave early today."

Ms. Delany nodded. Her brown eyes regarded Talli closely. "All right. The work on this one is easy. I think we have enough people here to handle everything."

"Okay," Talli said. "I guess I'll go, then."

Ms. Delany reached out and took her by the wrist. "Talli, I'm . . ." She shook her head and continued in a whisper. "Please be careful. I know Chris isn't telling me everything, and I'm scared. If anything happens to him . . ."

"We're being as careful as we can," Talli said. She smiled, but it did nothing to dent the look of concern on Donna's face.

At last Donna nodded and let go of Talli's wrist. "Take care of yourself, too," she said.

Talli hurried out of the auditorium and ran across the parking lot to her car. Clouds had come up to mask the sun, but the light was still uncomfortable. She shoved dark sunglasses over her eyes and drove away from the school. Talli still had no idea what she was going to tell Dr. Aston. She was sure that a psychiatrist heard weird stories every day, but she doubted that any of them were as weird as hers.

She also wasn't too sure she believed this doctor-patient confidentiality stuff. Talli didn't want any of her story getting back to her parents—or worse, to Lansky. Even if the psychiatrist wasn't supposed to tell anyone what Talli said, Talli was sure the doctor could convince everyone she was nuts.

She drove through the middle of town on her way to her appointment. The grand old houses along Main Street were still impressive, but something about them seemed bleak. After a moment Talli realized that it wasn't the houses that were different, it was her vision. Just as her nighttime vision was getting better and better, her daytime vision seemed to be getting duller. Colors and brightness were fading. Distance and depth were growing harder to make out.

Talli had a bad feeling. The seed of doubt that Chris had planted about Seth's energy was growing into full-blown suspicion. The energy had made her *feel* better, but she wasn't really getting better. In fact, she was becoming more a vampire—and less a human—all the time.

The psychiatrist's office was in the middle of a cluster of brick office buildings, wedged between a dentist's office and a place that sold expensive vacuum cleaners. For a second Talli thought about just driving on past, but there would be no getting around her parents if she did. So she parked near the door, took a deep breath, and went inside.

The waiting room didn't look very impressive. It was just a room with a desk and a couple of chairs that were about as fancy as the ones in Talli's living room. At the far end, bubbles percolated through an aquarium, where a cloud of silvery fish swam back and forth. There was no one behind the reception desk. After waiting a few seconds Talli walked around the chairs and peeked through the open door into the office. A red-haired woman wearing jeans and a turtleneck sweater was busy taking books from a box and stacking them on a shelf.

"Excuse me," Talli called. "I'm looking for Dr. Aston."

The woman turned around and smiled. "That's me," she said. "Are you Tallibeth McAlister?"

"Yes."

Dr. Aston brushed her hands against her jeans and turned her wrist to look at her watch.

"Good grief, it's time for your appointment right now," she said. She came over and shook hands with Talli. "Sorry if I left you standing in the waiting room. My secretary had to go out for a minute, and I didn't hear the door."

"That's okay," Talli said. "I just got here."

"Great," said the psychiatrist. "Come on in and have a seat." She walked across the room to a large hardwood desk and dropped into a chair behind it.

Talli looked around the office. There was nowhere to sit except for a pair of armchairs across the desk from Dr. Aston. "No couch?" she asked.

"Afraid not," Dr. Aston replied with a grin. "If I let my patients lie down, too many of them fall asleep on me."

Talli smiled. "You're not what I expected," she said.

Dr. Aston raised an eyebrow. "You were expecting a little old man with glasses and a beard, yah?" she asked with a mock German accent. Then she shook her head. "Look at your hair. I think you're the first patient I've ever had with hair redder than mine."

Talli winced. "Fire engines aren't as red as my hair," she said.

"It looks good," said the doctor. "Really. So many redheads get kind of orange. Yours is different. It's nice."

"Thanks," Talli said. She felt a blush creep into her cheeks at Dr. Aston's comments.

"By the way," said Dr. Aston, "my name is Joanne. Some patients like to call me that, some people stick with Dr. Aston. Whatever makes you feel comfortable is okay with me."

Talli was surprised to find that she did feel comfortable. She had expected this appointment to be very difficult to get through, but so far Dr. Aston was making it easy. "I guess I'll call you Joanne, if that's really okay. Oh, and everyone except my parents calls me Talli."

"Talli. Your name is as unique as your hair." Joanne picked up a small folder from the desk and pulled out a single sheet of paper. "I talked to your mother a couple of times. She tells me you were too sick to come in for your original appointment. I hope you're feeling better?"

"Yes," Talli said. She opened her mouth to say something more, but then she stopped. She still wasn't sure just how much she should tell this doctor.

"Well, I guess I don't have to tell you that your mother is very worried about you," Joanne said. "She's afraid that all the disappearances back in November have been awfully hard on you, and that you've changed."

I've changed more than she knows, Talli thought. "It is hard," she said aloud. "A lot of my friends are gone."

Joanne nodded. "The number of students missing is really alarming," she said. "I can't name any names, but quite a few students have been in to see me over the last couple of months. I've tried to tell the school board that there needs to be some counseling for all the students in the school, but they don't want to hear it."

"That sounds like our school board," Talli said. "School's really been a mess this year."

Joanne nodded. "So I understand. You know, it's too bad Principal Volker left. I only got to meet him once, but he seemed like someone who was willing to make some changes."

Talli shivered. "Yeah, he sure was."

"Didn't I see in the papers that he stopped some drug dealers at the school while he was there?"

"I was there when he did it," Talli said. "I—" She stopped and looked at Joanne with a frown. "Did my mother talk to you about this?"

The psychiatrist held up her hands and grimaced. "Caught red-handed," she said. "I was trying to be sneaky. Yes, your mother said you were still talking a lot about Volker, even though he'd been missing for a couple of months. She thought it was odd that you kept looking at his house and talking about him instead of your missing friends."

Talli looked into Joanne's hazel eyes. "That stuff about your not being allowed to tell anybody what I say. Is that serious?"

Joanne nodded. "Absolutely. I'd cross my heart, but I think you're a little too old for that."

She stood up and walked around the desk to sit in the chair next to Talli. "Nothing you say in here will ever go outside these walls. No one else will know. Not even your parents."

"Not the police?"

Joanne frowned. "No. Not the police."

Talli took a deep breath. "Volker was a monster," she said.

Joanne reached out and took one of Talli's hands. "Talli, did Principal Volker do something to you? Did he hurt you?"

"He tried to."

She squeezed Talli's hand. "Did he try to force you to do something you didn't want to do?"

A strangled laugh escaped Talli's lips. "No. No, it was nothing like that." She took a moment to settle her nerves and gather her breath. "What Volker tried to do was kill me."

"Why would he do that?" Joanne asked.

"Because I knew what he was," Talli said.

"A monster?"

"That's right." She looked away from Dr. Aston to the long wooden bookshelves that lined the walls. "All those kids that are missing? Volker killed them. And then I killed Volker."

Joanne released Talli's hand and leaned back in her leather chair. "Do you want to tell me about it?" she asked.

Talli shook her head. "I don't *want* to talk about it at all, but I think I have to." She closed her eyes for a moment to gather her thoughts. "It started when Volker came to town," she began.

She told about how Volker had moved into the empty house just two doors away from her. At first he seemed to be just what the school needed. He wanted to clean up the gangs and the drugs and make Westerberg High a place where people felt safe again. Everyone thought he was great. Everyone except Talli.

Right from the first day Talli thought there was something strange about Volker. Her boyfriend Alex and her friend Lisa had thought she was imagining things. It took a lot of convincing to get them to help her investigate Volker. Then kids started disappearing from the school.

One night Talli had tried to break into the principal's office to see what she could find, but Volker had scared her away. Lisa was supposed to pick up Talli at the school, but instead Talli had found the car empty—Lisa was gone. Talli had broken into Volker's home to look for Lisa, but Volker had come in and called the police. Finally Volker had tried to force Talli to become a monster like himself. She had escaped him at the school, leaving Alex behind.

After that there had been a terrible fight at Volker's house, in which Talli had killed several of the fledgling monsters Volker had created. Talli had gone to her parents for help, but Volker was able to control them, and they didn't lift a finger to stop him from attacking their daughter. In the end Talli had stabbed Volker in the neck with a silver corkscrew and watched him wither into nothing on her living-room floor.

All through the long story Dr. Aston sat with her hazel eyes locked on Talli. She asked a few questions, but not so many that Talli felt as if she were interrupting.

"And that was it until a few days ago," Talli said.

"What happened a few days ago?" Joanne asked.

"Alex came back."

"But I thought you said that Alex was dead."

"I did," Talli said. "And if you believe Chris, the real Alex *was* dead. What came back was another thing like Volker—another vampire. It was Alex who killed most of the people who disappeared last week. Except for Casey Pays. Alex turned Casey into a vampire, too, and Chris had to kill her."

Dr. Aston was sitting very still. Her forehead was creased in concern. "Is that it?" she asked.

Talli bit her lip and nodded. "Now you're going to tell me how crazy I am, right?"

"Well." Joanne grimaced and leaned back in her chair. "You're telling me that some vampires came to town and killed more than a dozen people, and then you killed the vampires. Is that right?"

"It does sound crazy," Talli said. "I know it does. But it's true."

"I could tell you one of those things they teach at the university. I could say that truth is relative, or that if it's true for you, that's all that matters." She stopped and shook her head. "But I don't believe that, and I don't think it's what you want to hear."

Talli's heart sank. She had known Dr. Aston for only a short while, but she had trusted her with more details about what had happened than anyone else, even Chris. "You think I imagined it all," she said in a dull voice.

"Not completely," Joanne said. "I think something happened. Probably something very disturbing."

"But not vampires."

"I don't believe in vampires." The psychiatrist leaned forward and took Talli's hand again. "Maybe if we work together, we can find out what really happened."

"I already told you what really happened," Talli said. "Everything happened just like I said it did, and it's still happening."

"Still happening?" Joanne frowned. "What does that mean?"

"I'm turning into a vampire," Talli said. "Right now, if I was to step over to your window, the sun . . ."

She stopped talking and stared out the window in surprise. It was dark out. Sometime while she had been telling her story, the sun had set and night had come on. Talli had been so involved in talking about the past months that she hadn't even noticed the sunset. "How long have I been here?" she asked.

Dr. Aston glanced at her watch. "About two and a half hours," she said. "I didn't want to interrupt you while you were telling me your story."

Talli felt a flush rise in her cheeks, but this time there was anger as well as embarrassment. "I appreciate your letting me talk, but it's not a 'story,'" she said. "It's what happened." She tried to think of something—anything—that would prove what she said was true. "Just ask Chris. He'll tell you what happened."

"Is this the same Chris that killed Casey Pays?"

"Yes. No!" Talli shook her head. "Chris says that since Casey was a vampire, she was already dead."

"Does that mean that you're dead, too?" Dr. Aston asked.

"I'm not a vampire," Talli said. "Not all the way. But I'm turning into one."

"I see." The psychiatrist reached for the sheet of paper on her desk and looked down at it for a moment. "Talli, one of the concerns your mother had was that you watch too many horror movies and read a lot of horror books. Do you think this might have something to do with why you're seeing vampires in Wester-berg?"

Talli jumped up from her chair. "I'm seeing vampires because there are vampires!" she shouted.

Something deep inside her seemed to move. Suddenly she could see a dim green light pulsing all around the psychiatrist. The green light made her stomach twist with hunger. She needed to feed.

"I've got to go." Talli headed for the door, but Dr. Aston beat her to it.

"I'm sorry I didn't believe your story," she said. "I could have lied to you and said I did, but I don't think that's a good way for us to start out. Look, can you come back tomorrow afternoon right after school? I think it'll help if we talk some more."

The hunger was growing stronger. "I'll come back," Talli said. "Please, just let me go."

There was obvious worry on the psychiatrist's face, but she stepped aside. Talli shoved her way through the door and almost ran across the waiting room and out into the dark parking lot. *I've got to find Seth,* she thought. *I've got to find him fast.*

Sky waited outside the motel-room door until the noise had stopped. Then she knocked and used her key to go inside.

"I'm back," she said.

Seth looked up from his evening paper and nodded. "I heard you outside," he said. "What did you find out?"

"She went to school," Sky said. "I stayed with her through most of her classes. Nothing happened that seemed strange. I could tell that she was running low on energy this afternoon."

Seth smiled. "She'll be looking for me very soon. I suppose we should get ready to go out." He stood up and folded his paper. "Did you bring me what I asked for?"

Sky nodded. She held out a thin book. "Here's the yearbook."

"And the photos?"

"They're inside. Plenty of shots of Talli."

Seth took the book from her hand. "Sky, after all this time, I believe you are finally beginning to be worth something." He walked past her, pulling pictures from the book and examining them one at a time.

"After school Talli went to see a psychiatrist," Sky said.

Seth turned, one eyebrow raised in surprise. "Did she?" He laughed under his breath. "I'll bet that was very interesting."

He stepped over the body that lay in the middle of the floor. "I'm going to get dressed," he said. "Take care of this while I do." He nudged the body with his toe.

Sky looked at the pale face and the staring

eyes of the girl on the floor. "I saw this girl at school," she said.

"Did you?" Seth asked distractedly as he went through his clothes. "She should have listened to her parents when they told her not to talk to strangers."

Sky carried the body out to the car and put it in the trunk.

Seven

❧

Vampires cannot cross running water.

"Wrong," Chris whispered. There were rivers all around Westerberg, and Volker and Alex had crossed them just fine. Even between the house where Volker had lived and the school there were several small streams. It was one more piece of folklore that didn't match up with the real thing.

"You finding anything?" he asked Donna.

"Maybe," said his sister. She scribbled something down on the pad in front of her. "I'll let you know."

Chris turned back to the volume he was reading. It was hard to concentrate on the old books after having been questioned for almost an hour by Lansky. He was still trembling with anger at the idea that Lansky thought he was involved in his parents' death. Chris had spent weeks trying to find out who murdered his parents. It was the Chicago police who had given up, not he. The frustration of not being able to find his parents' killers was one of the reasons he had gotten involved in trying to solve the disappearances in Westerberg.

Now, according to Lansky, the Chicago police had reopened the file on his parents—so that they could investigate the possibility that he had something to do with it.

The pencil in his hand snapped.

Donna looked over at him. "It'll be all right," she said. "You didn't have anything to do with what happened to Mom and Dad. They'll find that out as soon as they check."

"I know," Chris said. "I know." He sighed and turned back to his book.

The problem with looking for a solution this way was that there wasn't one set of vampire legends, there were hundreds, and none of them seemed to describe creatures like the ones that had come to Westerberg. From eastern Europe there were the tales of undead corpses that wandered the night. From Greece there were vampires that stood outside houses and called for people to come out, ready to consume anyone who answered. From America, and China, and Africa, and Australia—every country had its own legends of creatures that lived in the night.

Chris was surprised to find that not one of

the old myths was even close to the vampire stories he had seen in the movies. The sophisticated vampire with his black cape and his ancient castle didn't seem to exist outside of Hollywood. Many of the original vampire legends talked about things that sounded more like witches or ghosts.

Most disappointing of all, there was nothing in the books that was even close to what Chris had seen. If the old stories and legends had been started by the same creatures who were causing the problems in Westerberg, then the people who had recorded all those stories hadn't done a very good job of checking their facts.

Donna slammed her book shut. "More of the same," she said. "Do you really think we're going to find anything here?"

"I don't know," Chris said. He picked up his notepad. "Let's look at what we've got so far. Water comes up in a lot of the stories, but as far as we know, it doesn't really have any effect."

"We certainly know that snow doesn't bother them," Donna said. "It's been snowing like crazy in this town ever since they got here."

Chris tapped his finger against the next item on the pad. "Coffins," he said. "A lot of these stories have vampires that sleep in coffins or graveyards. As far as we know, there's nothing to that, either."

Except that Talli did see something that attracted her to the graveyard, he thought. He didn't say anything. If he told Donna about the graveyard, he'd have to tell her about Seth. And Chris wasn't ready to admit to Donna that there were other vampires in town.

"Religious symbols," Donna said. "In a lot of these stories, vampires can't stand to be near crosses, or churches, or things like that."

Chris nodded. "That one's in a lot of movies, too. I haven't seen anything to say it's true, but I haven't tested it. It's worth keeping in mind."

"Sunlight is another problem," Donna said. "Alex got around in the daytime, and Volker must have, too."

"But sunlight burned Talli, and she said it even killed several of the vampires that Volker had made," Chris added.

His sister nodded. "It's a good thing Talli's getting better," she said.

"Uh, yeah." Chris didn't tell her that Talli could stand sunlight only because she was taking energy from a vampire. If he did, he knew she'd never let him see Talli again. Donna was right—this whole thing was getting to be one big mess of lies. Now he was even lying to her.

Donna stood up and stretched. "Can we go home now? I need to plan for tomorrow's classes."

"I guess so," Chris said. "I'm going to check the racks one more time."

He found the section where the books on mythology and superstition were shelved. There were a few other books on vampires, but when he thumbed through them, it seemed that they only went over the same useless material he'd already seen. He put the books back on the shelves and was about to leave when another book caught his eye. He slid the old leather volume down from its perch and looked at the yellowed pages.

The more he read, the more convinced he was that he was on the trail of learning something important. He tucked the book under his arm and headed back to the table. When he stepped out from the shelves, he was surprised to see that Talli was sitting at the table with Donna, exchanging whispers.

"Hi," she said softly as Chris walked up. "I got finished with my appointment and thought you might still be here. Donna says you haven't found much that—"

She stopped and tilted her head to one side. "What are you grinning about?"

"I think I figured something out," Chris said.

"Something that could help?"

"Maybe." He slid into a chair, and the three of them leaned their heads close together. "I don't think you're a vampire," Chris said.

Talli frowned. "Not all the way."

"Maybe not even part of the way," Chris said.

"Well, if you mean not a vampire like in the movies, then I guess you're right," she said. "But it's a lot easier to say vampire than it is to say 'somebody who sucks life out of other people and doesn't like the sunlight.'"

"Yeah," Chris said, "but maybe there's a better word." He put the old leather book on the table and slid it toward her.

Talli picked up the volume and looked at the cracked gold letters on the cover. "Shapeshifters?" she asked. "What is this?"

"Come on. Somebody with as many horror books as you have must have heard of werewolves."

She looked up at him in surprise. "What have werewolves got to do with anything?"

"I don't understand either," Donna said. "Nobody turned into a wolf."

"But people did change shapes," Chris said. He took the book from Talli's hand and flipped through the pages. "There are stories in here from all over the world. Not just were*wolves*, but weretigers, werebears, were—just about anything you can think of."

"So?" Talli asked.

"Excuse me," said a voice over Chris's shoulder. He turned to see the librarian staring down at him. "It's time to close," she said.

"Okay," Chris said. "We'll be done in just a second." He turned back to the others. "Can we go somewhere else to finish talking?"

Donna stood and gathered her things. "I need to get home and work," she said. "I'll let you two figure this out."

"I'll be home as soon as I can," Chris said.

Donna nodded. "Be careful," she said. "Both of you."

"I think she's starting to trust me a little more," Talli said as Donna left the library.

"You don't look much like a monster," Chris said. "At least not when your hair's combed." Talli stuck out her tongue in response.

He picked up the book on werewolves and ran back to the librarian's desk to check it out. Then he followed Talli out into the darkness. After a moment's debate they decided to head for the diner on the north edge of town. A five-minute drive in Talli's car, a dash across a snowy parking lot, and Chris was standing inside rubbing his cold hands.

"Pick yourself a seat," the waitress called from behind the counter. "We're not too busy tonight."

In fact, there was no one else in the place. As Chris slid into one of the red leather booths, he found it hard to believe that less than a week had passed since he and Talli had first come to this diner. In this same booth, she had told him about Volker, and what had happened back in November. Now it was his turn to talk.

"The vampire books don't match what's happening to you," he said.

"I know that," Talli replied. "We talked about this before."

"One of the things that doesn't match is how these vampires can change their shapes." He pulled the old book from his coat pocket and put it on the table. "If all those old vampire legends are from people who saw real vampires and just got things wrong, why not werewolves, too?"

Talli was quiet for a second, her eyes focused on nothing. "Volker turned into a monster once," she said. "He was just trying to scare me, but he could make himself look like something besides another person. And his assistant, Lynch, actually turned into something like a wolf."

"All right," Chris said. "So I might really be onto something."

The waitress came over and took Chris's order for dinner. The most Talli would go for was a glass of soda.

"You sure you can't eat something?" Chris asked again after the waitress was gone.

Talli shook her head quickly. "Sorry. Food just sounds horrible." She looked out the window at the dark town. "I wonder if Seth will really find us," she said. "Maybe we should go look for him."

Chris frowned. "This afternoon you were telling me you weren't sure about Seth."

She wrapped her arms around herself and shivered. "That was before the energy ran out," she said. "I need it, Chris. I really need it."

A new fear tightened in his chest as Chris listened to Talli. More than ever he was convinced that whatever Seth had given her, it carried a high price. "If some of the things in these books are right," he said, "it might make a difference."

"Besides changing shapes," Talli said, "I don't see anything that makes us like werewolves."

"Us?" Chris asked in surprise.

She shrugged. "You know."

The trouble was, he *did* know. Talli had talked before about feeling different at night. In the afternoon she had seemed afraid of Seth and of what he was doing to her. Now she was thinking of herself as a vampire, and she was in a hurry to get more of what Seth had to offer.

"There's more in this book than you might think," Chris said.

"I don't feel different when there's a full moon," Talli said, "and I haven't been cursed by any Gypsies, either."

"How much wolfsbane have you run into?" Chris asked, trying to make a joke out of it. Talli didn't look amused. "Anyway," he continued, "it doesn't matter, because real werewolves didn't do any of that stuff. All that full-moon and Gypsy stuff was made up for the movies. The werewolves in these old stories could change shape anytime they wanted, and some of them could change to almost any shape they wanted."

They were quiet for a moment as the waitress set their drinks on the table and walked away. Talli picked up her glass of soda. "That does

89

sound right," she said. "What about silver bullets?"

"Bullets aren't in the old stories," Chris said, "but silver is. That's one of the things that made me pick up this book in the first place. Silver's not even in the vampire legends; it's werewolves that were hurt by silver."

Talli took a sip from her glass, made a face, and put it down. "This tastes terrible," she said.

"There's one other thing that's important about werewolves," Chris said.

"What's that?"

"Vampires are supposed to be dead. They're moving around, but their soul—or whatever it is that makes you a human being—is gone." He stopped and took a long drink of cold water. "But with werewolves," he continued, "they're still alive. And if they're alive, maybe they can be cured."

"You really think there's a chance?" Talli asked.

"I think there's a chance," he said. "And I think your friend Seth probably knows more about it than he's told us."

"Knows more about what?"

Chris looked up to see Seth standing over them. In the light of the diner, his face looked tanned and healthy. His cheeks were thin, and his eyes dark. His wavy hair was perfectly combed.

"Sorry if I startled you," he said.

"We were going to look for you," Talli said. "We were talking about it."

"Really?" Seth said. He nodded at the empty seat beside Talli. "Would you mind if I join you?"

"Sure," Talli said before Chris could get a word out. She slid to the corner of the booth, and Seth sat down beside her.

He looked across the booth at Chris and gave him a thin smile. "I didn't mean to interrupt," he said. "Please go on with your conversation."

Chris stiffened with anger, but he forced himself to speak as calmly as he could. "I was just saying that I thought you might know a way to help Talli."

Seth's smile grew wider. "But I'm here to help her," he said. "Just like I helped her last night."

"I don't think that kind of help is good for her," Chris said.

"Really?" He turned to Talli. "You want my help, don't you?"

Talli's green eyes were fixed on Seth's thin face. "Yes," she said softly. "Yes, please."

The windows of the truck grew steamy. Coach Pays wiped them clean and leaned over the dashboard for a better view. He frowned. The man in the trench coat was sitting with the other two in the diner, but the coach hadn't seen him come in. He watched them sitting together, and wondered if they were planning some drug deal, or talking about kidnapping someone else's daughter.

His fingers went across the car seat to the pistol beside him. The metal grips felt good and solid. He wasn't going to wait forever while Howard Lansky and the rest of the cops carried on with their questions. With McAlister's daughter one of the suspects, he was sure they were trying to sweep it under the rug.

Right now Casey could be tied up somewhere, just waiting for him to get her loose. He didn't intend to let her down. When the Delany boy and his two friends came out, he would follow them again. And when he got them alone, Coach Pays would make them tell him what they'd done with his Casey.

Something moved at the edge of the dimly lit parking lot. Coach Pays squinted at the thin figure that stood at the edge of shadow. It was a girl, he thought. A tall, thin girl. She moved toward the diner, and the light from the windows spilled across her face. Coach Pays's breath caught in his throat.

"Casey," he whispered.

The girl looked across the parking lot and smiled. His pistol forgotten, Coach Pays jumped out of the truck and ran toward his daughter.

Eight

❧❧❧

"Yes," Talli said. "Yes, please."

Energy hung around Seth in a cloud of glowing mist. Talli could see it. She could hear it singing to her like the buzzing of a thousand bees. She could even feel it brushing against her skin as she sat beside him. She ached with the need to have some of that energy for her own.

Chris said something to Seth, but Talli barely heard him. She was watching the power that shone behind Seth's eyes and played along the sharp features of his face. "I can give you more energy now," he said. "If you're sure that's what you really want."

Far down inside Talli's mind, a little voice was screaming that this was wrong. The energy that Seth had given her had done far more than get her through the day. It had changed her in

93

many ways and was changing her more every minute. But that little voice was drowned out by the overwhelming need for what Seth had to offer. He held out his hand. Talli took it and held on hard as power surged into her fingers, scorched a path along her arm, and bathed her body in fire.

When the first jarring impact had passed, Talli found that her night vision had expanded again. Colors had grown deeper. Textures bolder. She looked across the table at Chris and caught her breath. She could see every strand of his hair. She could see the blood moving under his skin. She could see the muscles tense in his jaw as he opened his mouth to speak, and she read his words from the movements of his face and throat before the air passed his lips.

"Are you okay?" he asked. The sound of his voice rang and echoed in her hearing, the words tumbling together.

Talli felt like laughing. Of course she was okay. She was far more than okay. "I feel great," she said. "Better than ever."

Chris smiled, but Talli could see the tension in his face. The green glow that surrounded his body was tinted with a streak of pale gray. She watched it swirl around his head, coloring his features like a fog. "That's good," he said. "Can you give me a ride home now? It's getting late."

"We should stay and talk to Seth," Talli said.

"Don't let me keep you," Seth said. "We'll have time to talk later."

"I thought you were leaving town," Chris said quickly.

"We are," Seth replied. "But not until we have finished our business here."

"Volker is gone."

"We're not so sure," Seth said. He looked at Talli, and his voice grew warm. "Please, I don't want to alarm you, but we've found no signs that this Volker of yours left town. Do take care in case he's still lingering in the area."

"We'll be careful," Chris put in. He reached across the table and took Talli by the arm. "I really do need to get rolling."

Talli turned to Seth. "Will I need more energy tomorrow?" she asked.

Seth raised a slim finger to his lips and appeared to be considering her question. "Let's wait and see. Each time I work with you, your capacity grows. You may be able to make it more than one day."

"Good," Chris said.

Seth turned to him for a moment and smiled. "I'm glad to see your interest in her improvement, Mr. Delany."

"I don't think she is improving," Chris replied. "And how did you know my name?"

"How can I help unless I know who I'm helping?" he said. "While you two young people were busy at school, I was learning a few things,

95

too." Seth's teeth flashed again, so white they seemed lit by an internal fire. "I don't lie in a coffin and sleep all day, you know," he said.

Chris stared at him for a long second. Talli could see that he was upset, but she felt too good to share Chris's feelings. "Come on," he said to Talli at last. "Let's go home."

Talli stood. Chris walked across the tiled floor and paid for his mostly uneaten dinner. He beckoned to Talli as he started for the door, and she followed, but she could still feel the pull of Seth behind her.

"Give my regards to your sister," Seth called as Chris was about to step through the door.

Chris froze. His hand fell from the doorknob, and he stepped back. He turned to face Seth, and Talli could see that his face was beet-red with anger. "You stay away from my sister!" he shouted.

"Hey," called the waitress from behind the counter. "No fighting in here."

Seth sat with his hands folded in his lap and looked at Chris with his gray eyes. "The families of my friends have nothing to fear, Mr. Delany. Please keep that in mind."

Talli could see the muscles bunching in Chris's neck. In a moment he would rush across the restaurant and try to hit Seth. And if Seth was as strong and as fast as Volker had been, a moment later Chris would be dead. Talli stepped between them and put her hands on Chris's shoulders.

"Like you said," she told him, "let's go home."

He looked over Talli's shoulder for a moment, and she could feel his heart thumping against his ribs. Then he stepped back and shoved open the door. "I know you can still hear me," he said in a low voice. "You stay away from my sister or I'll . . . I'll show you what I've learned." He stepped out into the night. Talli took one last look back as she went through the door. Seth was no longer at the table. She turned around rapidly, but somehow he had vanished.

Chris was standing beside her car when she went outside. He didn't say anything as she unlocked his door and let him in, and the silence continued as they drove through town.

As it had on the previous night, Seth's energy had opened up whole new worlds to Talli's senses. New shades of color appeared to her eyes. Even over the sound of her own car she could hear trucks moving on the main highway almost five miles away, and animals stepping though the snow at the side of the road. It was as if each time she met with Seth, another layer of obstruction was peeled away.

She looked over at Chris. He was hunched down in his seat, his eyes half closed, with his arms crossed tightly over his chest. She knew he wasn't seeing any of the marvelous things she could now understand about the night. To him it was all meaningless darkness. She didn't even have the words to explain to him how wonderful it all was, and how incredible she was feeling. She felt sorry for him.

"He doesn't know who killed Volker," Chris said as Talli turned onto her street.

"What do you mean?" Talli asked. "I thought you told him Volker left so he wouldn't suspect us."

Chris shook his head. "He knew I was lying, but he's not sure what happened. If he knew for sure, he'd just kill us and get it over with. He's testing us. He's trying to get me to slip up and say something."

"Seth's not like that," Talli protested. "He's—"

"He's what?" Chris interrupted. "He's beautiful and wise and generous? Wake up, Talli. He's a vampire. Vampires kill people, and as soon as he learns what he wants from us, he'll kill us, too."

Talli pulled the car up to the curb in front of Chris's house. "I don't believe it," she said. "He's had plenty of chances to kill us if that's what he wanted. Seth's not like Volker. He's here to help."

Chris snorted. "Yeah, sure." He pushed open the door and stepped out into the snow. "Please," he said, "please don't let him give you any more energy until I've had time to find out some more things. Even if it means staying out of the sun all day. Just keep away from Seth. When he finds out what really happened to

Volker, there's no telling what he'll do."

"Seth wouldn't kill me," Talli said.

Chris stared at her for a long time. "Maybe you're right," he said at last. He leaned in and gave her a quick kiss. "I hope you are." Then he slammed the car door and slogged through the snow to his house.

Talli drove the short distance home and pulled into the driveway. Her father was waiting for her when she came into the kitchen.

"You're home late," he said. "Mom's over at your grandmother's, and I'm getting ready to ride over to Stroud City on business. You want anything to eat before I leave?"

"I went to the diner with some friends," Talli said. "I ate there."

Her father stepped closer. "Friends, eh? Was the Delany boy one of those friends?"

"No," Talli said, but she could feel something inside her break as she lied straight-out to her father. "Just some girlfriends," she added.

Her father nodded. "You stay away from Delany. I don't know what Lansky's up to, but he hasn't given up yet. Has he talked to you?"

She shook her head. "No, I haven't seen him."

He leaned in close and touched a big hand to Talli's cheek. "You sure you're getting enough to eat, sweetheart? You're looking peaked."

"Peaked?" Talli managed a small smile. "You sound like Grandma."

Her father scowled. "I do, don't I? Well, I'll be back in a couple of hours." He pushed open the kitchen door and let it swing shut behind him. A moment later Talli heard the engine of his truck as he left the driveway and headed off.

She wandered around the kitchen for a moment, pulling open drawers and cabinets, then shutting them again. Down in her guts the hunger was growing. The hunger she didn't know how to feed. The confidence that had come over her when she got the energy from Seth began to fade. She could still feel the fire burning through her, and all her senses were sharper than ever. But it wasn't enough. She needed more. And she didn't need it tomorrow, or the next day—she needed it now.

Sleep, she thought. *I'll get some sleep, and when the sun's up, I'll feel different.*

She went up the stairs to her room, not bothering to turn on any lights in the dark house as she went. Talli peeled off her clothing and stretched in the darkness of her room. She had a sudden mad urge to run outside just as she was. The cold didn't hurt her any longer, and no one else would be able to see her in the night. She brushed the thought aside, pulled out an oversize football jersey, and slid into it. Talli wasn't at all tired, but she lay down on the bed and tried to push the hunger away.

What happened next wasn't clear. She remembered going to the window, but she didn't remember opening it, and she certainly didn't remember climbing down the steep snow-covered roof to the ground. But she must have done it, because the next thing she knew, Talli was standing knee-deep in the snowdrifts in her dark backyard.

Seth stepped out of a clump of pines and walked slowly toward her. "Are you ready?" he asked. His voice was as soft and dark as black velvet.

Ready for what? Talli wondered, but she nodded. She could feel the tingle of the snow against her bare feet and legs, and the north wind biting though her thin night shirt. But those things didn't hurt her. What did hurt was the hunger that raged through her and threatened to tear her apart. "Help me," she whispered.

Seth turned and beckoned toward the trees. From the darkness beneath them stepped Grant Winchell. His eyes were half-closed, and his mouth gaped open. Like a puppet on strings, he staggered across the snow-covered lawn and stood swaying beside Seth. All around Grant, Talli could see the brilliant green cloud of his life energy.

"You're hungry," Seth said.

"Yes," whispered Talli. She couldn't take her eyes off Grant. The energy called to her. All her thoughts were drowning under the roar of her hunger.

101

Seth put his hands on Grant's shoulders and pushed him toward Talli. "Take him," he said.

Isn't that wrong? she thought. "You said I couldn't," she stammered. Just finding the words was difficult.

"Take him," Seth repeated.

Talli reached up and touched Grant's face. He moaned, and his head rolled on his neck. A spark of green fire leaped between Grant's dark skin and the end of Talli's finger. In a second the spark had become a crackling stream that thickened into a twisting ribbon of light. Talli closed her eyes. She wasn't just pulling in the energy, she was living in it—riding every wave and surge of power. For a moment it seemed that this euphoria might never end, but it did.

Talli blinked and staggered back. Grant was lying in the snow, his skin gray and dull. "Is he dead?" she asked.

"No," Seth said. "It wouldn't do to have another unexplained death tonight." He stepped closer to Talli. "Now you know," he said, putting his arm around her waist. He felt as solid and strong as stone as he pulled her close. He bent down, and Talli felt his warm breath against her throat. "Now you know," he whispered in her ear.

Talli leaned against him and tried to catch her breath. She didn't have to ask what Seth meant. Now she knew what she really was.

Sky was sitting on the kitchen counter when

Seth came in. She was swinging her long legs, letting her heels drum against the front of a wooden cabinet. "We've got a guest," she said.

"So I see," Seth replied. He took off his trench coat, tossed it across the table, and looked around the room at the worn furniture and framed sports photographs. "I take it that he's the owner of this house?"

Sky nodded.

"I'm afraid I can't say I approve of your taste in housing," he told Sky. He leaned down to look at the bony face of the man sitting numbly at one end of the table. "Can't say much of your taste in prey, either."

"He was outside the diner tonight," Sky said. "He was following your redhead."

Seth raised a thin eyebrow. "Really?" He pulled out a wooden chair, turned it around, and sat down on it backward. "And who are you?" he asked.

"Pays," mumbled the man.

"I saw him at the school," Sky said. "He's the coach for their football team." She picked up the school yearbook from the counter and held it out for Seth to see. "Remember the girl I showed you in here last night, the one that's missing? It's his daughter."

"Well," Seth said, "isn't that interesting?" He put his hand on the man's chin and turned his head to look into his dark-blue eyes. "You think this one is out to do our new friends some harm?"

"There was a gun in the truck," Sky said.

"A gun? How very dangerous." Seth smiled at Coach Pays. "You know, in a way, I'm a coach myself."

"Coach," repeated Pays.

"That's right," Seth said. "I'm Coach Seth, and I think I'd like to have you on my team." He patted the tall man on the shoulder. "We have too many players on the field, and I need to get rid of one of them."

"Get rid of one," Pays said.

"Absolutely," Seth cried. "You know the boy, the one called Christopher Delany?"

"Delany."

"Yes! You catch on quick, Pays. Well, he's the one that made your daughter . . ." He stopped and snapped his fingers.

"Casey," Sky said.

"My Casey," Pays said.

"Ah, yes," Seth said, shaking his head sadly. "Delany's the one that made your little Casey go away."

A spark appeared in Coach Pays's dark eyes. "Get rid of Delany," he said.

"Yes. That's it, get rid of Delany." Seth leaned back in his chair and put his feet up on the battered table. "You get rid of him, and then I won't have to do it."

"Why kill him?" Sky asked. "We'll be gone soon, and what's he going to say?"

Seth's smile grew thin. "Getting a soft heart,

Sky? Delany is trying to stop Talli from coming to me. He even wants to turn her back into a green. We can't have that."

"Turn her back?" Sky said in surprise. "That's not possible, is it?"

"No," Seth said. "Of course not. Talli's one of us now, and she always will be."

Nine

❧❦❧

Wednesday

Chris held the clove of garlic to his nose and sniffed. "Whew!" he said. "It would sure repel me. Especially before breakfast."

Donna plucked it out of his fingers and smelled it herself. "It's not so bad," she said, "and it's in a lot of the books."

"So what do you think we should do?" Chris asked. "Eat it for lunch?"

"That probably wouldn't hurt," said his sister, "but I was thinking more about making a pendant out of it."

"Great. So I'm going to wear a big chunk of garlic around my neck and go all over town smelling like a bowl of spaghetti?" He shook his head. "I don't think so."

Donna slid into her coat and pulled her book bag over her shoulder. "You're the one who had me looking up ways to get rid of vampires," she said. She looked in her bag and frowned, then began looking under the junk mail stacked on the counter.

"I don't want to get rid of Talli," Chris replied. "I want to cure her."

"Well, I didn't come across anything about curing vampires."

Chris frowned. "Neither did I," he said. "I thought I was onto something when I found the book on werewolves, but I haven't found anything helpful yet."

Donna looked up in disgust. "Okay, where are the keys?"

Chris grinned. Donna had a photographic memory—she saw something once and never forgot it. But all her life she'd been losing the car keys.

"They're on the counter by the door," Chris said. He followed Donna outside and climbed into the car. The sun was shining through gaps in the clouds, and Westerberg had regained something of its winter magic. Chris looked over at Talli's house as they went past. The daylight made his fears seem less real, but he was still worried about her.

Seth was up to something, but Chris didn't know what. As they drove through town, Chris wondered if he should tell Donna about Seth. He didn't want to scare her, but she was very smart—having her help would be worth a lot. He opened his mouth to speak, but Donna beat him to it.

"It's a shame you said all the stuff in the movies doesn't mean anything," she said.

"Why?" Chris asked.

Donna turned into the school parking lot and glided into a slot. "Because," she said, "I saw a werewolf movie once where someone got cured."

"You did? How?"

"He killed the guy that made him a werewolf," she said, "and that broke the curse."

Chris's mouth fell open. "You're right. I've seen that in films, too." He shook his head in wonder. "Sometimes that perfect brain of yours comes in handy."

"Always happy to help." She gathered her things and pushed the car door open. "But remember, you said that the movies were all wrong."

Chris stared at the brick side of the school building and tried to think. "Yeah, I did." Donna slammed her door and walked away from the car. Chris sat for a few seconds longer, then climbed out and hurried after her. "Alex is dead," he said, "and Talli's still getting worse."

"There you go," said his sister. "The movies are wrong."

"Yeah," Chris admitted, "but maybe partly right. Silver works, so maybe there's something to this."

Donna paused with her hand on the school door. "We've got another negative example. Alex stayed a vampire after Volker died."

Chris scowled. "Sometimes that perfect brain of yours can really be a pain," he said. Donna laughed and went inside.

Through the morning Chris wondered if there was any hope in what Donna had said. If he remembered the story, werewolves were supposed to track down and kill the werewolf who had created them. But Alex was dead, and Volker was dead. So if the theory was true, Talli should be back to normal. Still, there was something about the idea that nagged at him. It was the closest thing he had to a clue, and he didn't want to give it up.

He looked for Talli at lunchtime. Usually she came in a few minutes after he did, and he kept expecting her to show up while he was in line for his food. But this time he made it to the end of the line and paid for his food, and there was still no sign of her. He walked through the crowded cafeteria and found a spot at the end of a long table. As he picked at the lunchroom food, he looked around the room, hoping to catch a glimpse of Talli's red hair shining through the crowd.

"Where's your girlfriend?" said a voice from behind him. Chris turned to see Paul Katz standing over him. Katz lived in one of the few houses between Chris and Talli. His nickname around school was "Katz the Rat," and he always seemed to have some piece of dirt to tell. What he'd told Chris about Volker had helped Chris figure out what was going on in Westerberg. But that didn't mean Katz was friendly. In fact, when Lansky talked about a neighbor's saying Casey was at the Delanys' the night she vanished, Chris suspected that it was Katz who'd blabbed.

"She must not be hungry," Chris said.

Katz sat next to Chris without asking and began to shovel down a plateful of some unidentifiable casserole. "People are talking about you two," he said between bites.

"They are? What are they saying?"

"They're saying you did something to Casey Pays," he said. "They're saying the police are after you."

"That's what other people are saying?" Chris asked. "Or is it what you're saying?"

"If I were you, I'd be worried about what the police are saying," Katz said. "Especially now, after what happened to Grant."

"Grant who?"

Katz looked up from his plate and chewed slowly. "Maybe your girlfriend knows," he said.

Chris pushed away from the table and walked out of the cafeteria. He didn't know who Grant was, but he could guess what had happened to him—he was either missing or dead. Chris walked down the hall to Donna's room and found her at her desk grading papers. "Hi

111

Was Talli in your class this morning?"

Donna looked up and frowned. "No. I was going to ask you if you knew why."

Chris shook his head and backed out of the room. Talli had gotten the energy she needed to go out during the day, but she still wasn't at school. And the way Katz was talking, it seemed some other strange things were going on, too. Chris started down the hallway, unsure of what to do or where to go. Ten steps along, he suddenly turned around and headed back to get the car keys from Donna. He didn't care if it was the middle of the day, he was going to go home and check on Talli.

A strong arm went around his throat and a hand clapped down over his face. Before Chris even had time to draw a breath, he was pulled out of the hall into a pitch-black storage room. He kicked back and felt his heels bounce off someone's legs. Then he reached back with his arms to try to grab whoever was holding him, but the arm around his neck tightened and his vision turned gray.

"Don't move," said a soft voice. "If you'll just be still, I'll let go."

Chris struggled for a moment longer, then forced himself to be still. After a second the crushing pressure on his throat eased. He fell away from his attacker and pulled in a lungful of cool air. "Who are you?" he asked as soon as he felt well enough to speak.

There was a soft click, and a row of fluorescent tubes flickered to life overhead. A black-eyed girl stood by the door. "It's me," she said. "Sky."

Chris stared at her. He wasn't sure that he would have recognized her again—in the darkness of the graveyard two nights before, he'd gotten only an impression of tallness. He hadn't even been certain that she was a girl. She was.

Many times Chris had heard people described as having a heart-shaped face, but he never met anyone who fit that description as well as Sky. High cheekbones underlined wide black eyes. Her hair, which had looked simply black in the night, was a warm brown shot through with highlights of gold and auburn. She didn't have a typical homecoming-queen prettiness. Her nose was too long and thin, and her mouth too wide for that kind of magazine perfection. Like Talli, her features were unique. Like Talli, she wasn't really pretty—but she was beautiful.

"What do you want?" he asked.

She tilted her head to one side and looked at him critically. "You really think it's possible?" she asked.

"I don't understand," he said.

"A cure," Sky said. "You think you can cure her?"

Chris rubbed at his sore neck and tried to think. "If you mean Talli," he said, "then I don't know. I'm trying."

Sky nodded. "You better come up with something fast, because Schelling is way ahead of you."

"Who's Schelling?"

"That's his name, Seth's real name. Or at least it's the oldest name of his I know." She shrugged her thin shoulders. "He's always making up new names."

"Has he got Talli?" Chris asked. "She hasn't been at school today."

"Depends on what you mean by 'got,'" Sky said. "I don't think he's holding on to her, but I think he's already got her ready to do whatever he says." She leaned back against a metal rack of worn basketballs. "Schelling came to town to find Volker. Since he can't have Volker, he plans to take your Talli."

So many questions sprang to mind that Chris had a hard time asking any of them. "What does he want with Talli?"

"I told you," Sky said, "he really came for Volker."

"Then why did he want Volker?" he asked. "I bet it didn't have anything to do with protecting the people in this town."

Sky smiled, and her wide mouth was bracketed by dimples. "You got that right. Schelling couldn't care less if everyone in this town fell down a well. No, he's just collecting others. Schelling's getting old enough to want a city of his own."

"I still don't understand. How can he have a city?"

"He wants a city for a hunting ground. When a dozen people disappear in a town this size, people start calling it a disaster." She reached into the rack and picked up one of the basketballs. "When a dozen people disappear in the city, they just call it a week." With one hand she squeezed the basketball. It bulged between her fingers, then popped like a stuck balloon.

Chris looked at the limp basketball as Sky dropped it to the floor. Sky looked thin and fragile, but he had no doubt she could break him in half if she tried. "That still doesn't tell me why he was after Volker."

"Do I have to spell it out?" Sky asked. "Cities have lots of vampires, and they all have their territory. If Schelling's going to get some space, he needs some others to help him out. That's why he's got me, and that's why he wants Talli."

"He's building an army," Chris said in surprise.

"More like a family."

"Is Grant Winchell part of that family?"

Sky stared at him blankly. "Who's Grant Winchell?"

"He's another student," Chris said. "Somebody asked me about him, and I think he's missing."

"No matter what saintly lines Seth's feeding your girlfriend, he still likes a little snack now and then." She shrugged. "I wouldn't doubt that this Winchell was last night's dinner."

Chris thought about that for a second; then he decided to ask the question that was bothering him the most. "So why are you telling me all this?"

Sky's dark eyes looked him up and down. "Tell me the truth. Can you do something to turn Talli back?"

"I'm not sure," Chris said. "I think I've got an idea, but I don't know how to test it."

"But there's a chance?"

"Yeah, I think there's a chance."

Sky looked around as if she were making sure the room was empty and the door was still shut. "Could you change me back?" she asked.

Chris didn't know what to say. His idea was no more than a hunch, and probably a hunch that was wrong. But if he could get Sky on his side, he might stand a chance against Seth. "If it works for Talli, it'll probably work for you, too," he said.

"I wish I could believe that," Sky said. She closed her eyes and brushed back her brown hair. "I should probably just kill you now. If I wait, Seth will find out that I talked to you, then he'll be after me."

"Wait," Chris said. "I may not be sure about how to turn you back, but I know how to keep Seth from hurting either you or Talli."

"How?"

"We kill him first."

Sky laughed. "You don't know what he's like. I'm twice as strong as any normal person, but he's ten times as strong as me. He'd kill you before you put a scratch on him." She shook her head. "Killing a vampire's not as easy as you think."

Chris could almost feel his life hanging in the balance. If he said the wrong thing, it could cost both him and Talli everything. "I've already seen two die," he said. "And that was without you to help."

Sky was very still for a moment; then she started to nod slowly. "Seth already figures that you killed Volker. If he knew for sure, he'd turn you inside out and use your skull for a football."

"Think about it," Chris said. "Wouldn't you like to be free of him?"

"More than anything," she said. A bell rang in the hallway outside to signal the end of lunch hour. "Get back in your classes and don't tell anyone you talked to me—especially not your dear little Talli."

"Talli's okay," Chris said. "She's on our side."

Sky pushed open the door and peeked out. "Wrong on both counts," she said. "Talli's a long way from okay, and she's been on Seth's team from the moment she took his energy."

She glanced back at Chris, then stepped outside and was gone. He stayed inside the storage room for a second, trying to make sense of

117

everything he'd heard. As Chris had suspected, everything Seth had told them had been a lie. He was in town to create a family of vampires, and Talli was going to be part of it.

Even if Chris figured out a way to cure Talli now, it would probably mean that Seth would just kill them both. The only solution was what he had said to Sky: they would have to kill Seth.

Something Chris had heard about sports came to mind: the best defense was a strong offense. He hoped whoever made that one up knew what he was talking about.

Coach Pays saw the boy walking down the hallway and smiled. It was nice to know that he was the one. This was the one to blame. And when this boy was dead, everything would be just fine again. Everything would be better than ever.

He smiled again as the boy walked past. *Very soon*, he thought. *Very soon now.*

As soon as he was given the word, the boy would be dead.

All it took was one word from the coach. Then the boy would be dead, and everything in the world would be fixed.

Ten

❧❧❧

Talli opened her eyes. The sun was still leaking in around her curtains. She snarled at it. Not because it hurt, but because the sun was her enemy. She didn't have to think about it, that was just the way things were. She looked around the small room to see who had disturbed her daytime rest. Posters from horror films looked back at her, but nothing moved in the dimly lit bedroom. Good. She needed her rest. She turned over and closed her eyes.

A sound came again. It took Talli a moment to realize that it was the sound that had woken her up in the first place. It took her even longer to figure out that the sound was coming from a small white thing nearby. She reached across the bed and slapped the white thing. It fell from its perch and bounced on the wooden floor. The noise stopped. Talli gave a satisfied growl. Now she could go back to resting.

"Hello?" said a tiny, distant voice. "Talli? Are you there?"

Talli looked down at the white thing. It wasn't dead. She would have to make sure this time. She rolled to the edge of the bed and reached down to pick it up. She squeezed, and there was a sharp crack as the shell of the thing began to split.

"Talli, what's going on?" said the thing.

Talli grinned. One more squeeze, and she would crush this thing that had a voice like Chris.

Chris.

Something like a pane of glass shattered in Talli's mind. She snapped awake and scrambled to turn the phone around and hold it up to her ear. "Chris?" she called. "Are you still there?"

"Talli, are you all right?" he asked.

"Yes, I'm . . ." She stopped and pulled in a deep breath. "No, I'm not all right. It's like my brain's been switched off. I don't remember much of anything last night after I dropped you off."

"It's that energy that Seth's been feeding you," Chris said. "It's doing strange things to you."

"Without that energy I'd be stuck hiding from the sun."

"So where are you now?" Chris said.

Talli rubbed her tired eyes. "Good point. But it's not much of a choice. I take the energy, and I feel strange, or I don't take the energy and I feel worse."

"There's more to what Seth is doing than just feeding you energy," Chris said. "I had a talk with Sky today."

"With who?"

"Sky. The girl who was with Seth in the graveyard, remember?"

"I remember," Talli said. "What was she doing talking to you?"

"She met me at school today, she told me all about why Seth's really here. I need to come over and talk to you."

Talli found the clock on the nightstand. "It's almost five now, but you probably have time to come over before my mom or dad gets home."

"Great," he said. "I'll be right over."

"Wait," Talli said. "I just thought of something. I'm supposed to go back and see Dr. Aston this afternoon. In fact, I should be over there already."

"How about I ride over with you?" Chris asked. "I don't want you to be alone."

Talli stretched the phone cord to its limits as she looked through her closet for something to wear. "You better not," she said. "It's an hour appointment, and last time we went longer than that. You'd just be stuck waiting for me outside."

"Well, be careful," he said. "If what Sky told

me is true, there's a lot more going on than we thought. I'll meet you at my house as soon as you're back."

"Okay," Talli said. "I'll see you then."

"And be sure and get away if you run into Seth," Chris added.

"I'm going to have to talk to him sometime," she said. "I need the power."

"Please, stay away from him. Wait until you hear what I've learned."

"I've really got to go," Talli said. "Back as soon as I can." She found a sweater and some jeans and slipped into them as fast as she could. She glanced in the mirror and frowned at her pale face. It looked as if she'd been hiding from the sun for a year, not just a day. A few strokes with a brush made her hair look a little less like a rat's nest. She sat on the edge of the bed and pulled on her boots; then she grabbed her coat and purse and headed for the door.

As Talli was getting into her car, she looked up at the western sky and frowned. The sun was setting behind a wall of heavy gray clouds. It looked as if more snow was on the way. Something bad seemed to happen every time it snowed. The final battle with Volker had come during one of the first snows of the season, and the last night with Alex had been during the biggest snow in years. Talli tried to tell herself that it was only coincidence, but looking up at the approaching storm, she couldn't help feeling that something more than snow was on its way.

By the time she got to Dr. Aston's office, the sky was a dark bruised purple. She hurried across the parking lot and pushed open the door to the waiting room. A sandy-haired man was seated behind the receptionist's desk. He looked up as Talli came in. "Are you Tallibeth McAlister?" he asked.

She nodded. "Sorry I'm late."

The blond man smiled. He was very good-looking and seemed a little familiar. Talli thought that maybe he had been only a year or two ahead of her in school.

"Dr. Aston's on the phone right now," he said. "Have a seat, and she'll be ready for you in just a minute."

"Thanks." Talli sat down in one of the leather chairs and dropped her purse on the table. She pushed around the stack of magazines, but nothing caught her eye. It was hard to get too interested in fashion or celebrities when you were turning into a vampire. She leaned back and looked at the fish swimming lazily around in the aquarium. She had heard that watching fish was supposed to be relaxing, but all she could think was that they looked as trapped as she felt.

"Okay," said the guy at the desk. "She's off the phone. Go on in."

"Thanks again," Talli said. She picked up her things and went into the office.

Dr. Aston met Talli just inside the door. "Glad to see you made it back," she said. "I always know I wasn't too awful when a patient makes it for a second visit."

Instead of the casual clothes she had worn the day before, Dr. Aston had on a soft green dress and a silver necklace. She caught Talli's gaze and smiled. "You'll have to excuse me for being fancied up tonight. I've got a date."

"I hope I'm not keeping you too late," Talli said.

"Absolutely not. Come on, let's get started." Dr. Aston picked up a notepad and a folder from the top of her desk, and she and Talli took their places again in the soft chairs.

"I'm not sure what else to say," Talli started. "If you won't believe me, what good does it do to talk?"

Dr. Aston frowned. "It's not that I don't believe you, Talli. It's just that I don't believe in vampires."

"I do."

"I know you do," Dr. Aston said. "But it's my job to find out why you believe in them, and to see if we can find out what's behind your belief."

"I believe in them because they're real," Talli said flatly.

Dr. Aston glanced down at the papers in her lap. "Let's try this," she said. "Yesterday you were telling me that you thought you were turning into a vampire yourself."

"I am," Talli said. "It gets worse every day."

"Okay." Dr. Aston closed the folder and leaned forward in her chair. "So tell me how this happened. Was it Principal Volker who made you a vampire?"

Talli shook her head. "No, it was Alex."

"Alex?"

"Alex Cole. He was my boyfriend, then Volker made him into a vampire. I thought he was dead, but last week he came back and he tried to take me away with him."

"I see," Dr. Aston said. "So Alex is one of the students who everyone else thinks ran away?"

"That's right, but he didn't."

"Is he still around?"

"No," Talli said. "He's dead."

Dr. Aston's eyebrows went up and lines of tension appeared in her forehead. "How can you be sure?"

"He attacked me," Talli said. "We fought, and I left him in Volker's house. The house burned, and Alex didn't come out. He must be dead."

"Were you the one who burned down the house?" Dr. Aston asked.

"No, it was an accident. Alex . . ." Talli stopped and pulled in a deep breath. "I'm sorry," she said, "but this is really frustrating. I don't like talking about this. You don't believe me. And even if I tell you the whole story, you're just going to try to make something else out of it."

"I'm not going to lie to you, Talli," Dr. Aston said. "I don't believe in vampires, and I don't think I ever will. I think something happened to you, something that you may not want to remember. To protect you from the memory of whatever happened, your mind has reached back to the horror books and movies that you like and pulled out vampires as a way to explain what's happened."

"I think I should leave," Talli said. "I don't think this is going to be any fun for either one of us."

"Therapy isn't always fun," Dr. Aston said, "but sometimes it's necessary. Your view of the world is different from that of everyone else. We've got to—"

"Wait," Talli said. "What if I show you it isn't?"

Dr. Aston shook her head. "Show me?"

Talli nodded. "I can bring in someone else who'll tell you that at least part of my story is true."

"I don't think we should do that," Dr. Aston said.

"But if I have someone else," Talli said, "won't that prove I'm telling the truth?"

Dr. Aston bit her lip; then she nodded. "Maybe it would help. Is this another student you're talking about?" she asked.

"That's right. He's only been in town about two weeks, but he knows about Alex. He saw

Alex, and he saw Casey Pays, and—"

"Casey Pays?" Dr. Aston leaned away from Talli. "Isn't she the girl who's missing? The one everybody's asking about?"

"Yeah," Talli said. "Alex turned her into a vampire."

"Talli, this is very important. If you know where Casey Pays is, you have to tell."

Before Talli could reply, the door to the office swung open, and the blond receptionist come walking in with a grin on his handsome face. "Hi," he called. "Mind if I join you?"

Dr. Aston looked at him in surprise. "Bryan, we're in the middle of a session."

His smile widened. "I'm not sure that I've seen two such lovely redheads in the same room before," he said. "Quite a treat."

Dr. Aston stood up. "Bryan, get out of here right this second."

The sun went down. Talli could feel the moment of its setting as if a giant switch had been thrown. Instantly, all the colors in the room changed. Textures grew sharper and a swirl of green streaked with red appeared around Dr. Aston. Talli looked at the man standing in the door. Instead of a green glow, he was surrounded by a bright, pulsing light of all colors.

"Bryan, if you want to save your job," Dr. Aston said firmly, "you had better leave this office right this instant and never interrupt me with a patient again."

"That's not Bryan," Talli said softly.

The man walked across the room and perched on the corner of the desk. "I've been listening," he said. "I'm a good listener. But I don't think you're doing a very good job of listening, Doctor."

Dr. Aston's face had turned red with anger. "Bryan, you're fired. Now get out of here before I call the police."

"That's not Bryan," Talli said more insistently. She stood up and turned to face the intruder.

"Please, Talli," Dr. Aston said. "Let me handle this."

The man on the desk shook his head and put on an expression of mock sadness. "There you go again. Talli tells you the truth and you don't want to listen."

Talli took Dr. Aston by the arm and pulled her back. "Get out of here," she said.

"I'm afraid it's too late for that," said the man. His features swam and flowed like melting candle wax. Black shot from the roots of his hair to the tips. In a moment the man on the desk was no longer Dr. Aston's receptionist. It was Seth.

"Hello, Doctor," he said. "Are you starting to believe?"

Dr. Aston's face had gone from the red of anger to the pale gray of shock. She staggered back half a step. "Who are you?" she choked out.

"He's a vampire," Talli said. "He's come here for me."

"For you," Seth said. "And for dinner." He opened his mouth to reveal a pair of comically long fangs. "What do you think, Doc? Do you believe her now?"

Dr. Aston trembled violently and leaned against one of the chairs for support. "You're not real," she said. "You can't be."

The fangs in Seth's mouth shrank back to normal teeth. "You'll have to excuse me. Those are good for show, but they make it difficult to talk." He smiled again and rubbed his hands together briskly. "Now, what's real and what's not. I'm afraid it's your neat, cozy, well-lighted little world that's not real, Doc. The real world has lots of dark corners, and lots of dark things live in them."

Talli glanced toward the door. Dr. Aston would never make it out of here. Seth was too fast. But if Talli ran, she might at least be able to make it to the phone on the front desk.

"Get out of here," Dr. Aston said. She picked up the phone on her desk. "I'm calling the police."

Seth shook his head. "Tsk, tsk, tsk. Aren't you always trying to get people to face up to reality, Doc? Now reality has come to visit, and you don't even want to look."

Talli ran for it. She took two steps before something knocked her against the wall. There was a blur of movement, and for a disorienting moment the world turned upside down. When things were still again, Talli was back in one of the leather chairs, and Seth was back in his spot on the desk.

"Don't worry, dear, we'll be leaving shortly," he said. "As soon as we've taken care of the good doctor."

"Leave her alone," Talli said. "She's got nothing to do with this."

"She didn't have anything to do with it before you talked to her," Seth said. "But now she knows far too much, doesn't she?"

"I'll do what you want," Talli said. "Just leave the people in this town alone."

"You'll do what I want," Seth said, "because you're hungry."

Talli shook her head. "I'm not."

"You're hungry," Seth repeated.

"I'm—" Talli threw back her head and screamed. The hunger wasn't a feeling anymore, it was a beast that raged through her body. Every nerve, every muscle, every bone cried out for energy. "Make it stop!" she begged. "Please make it stop."

Seth slid off the desk and walked slowly over to Talli. "I'll help you," he said. He ran his fingers through Talli's hair and gently touched her face. "Did you know there's more than one way to pull energy from these pitiful greens? When a new gold, like you, draws out the energy, there's enough for only a day or two. But an experienced gold, like myself, has other tricks."

He gave Talli a last comforting smile; then he whirled around, seized Dr. Aston by the chin, and squeezed her mouth open between his thumb and forefinger. He raised her one-handed, holding her by the face, with the ease of a child holding up a rag doll, until her feet dangled above the ground. Her fingers clawed at his grip, and her feet hammered against his legs, but Seth didn't seem to notice.

He tilted his head to the side and looked at her with apparent sympathy. "You really are a lovely woman, Doctor. I'd like to take you out and show you the real world. Really, I would. But my friend here is very hungry, and now, I think, it's suppertime." He put his face very close to Dr. Aston's, opened his mouth, and took a long, deep breath.

A moan whistled through Dr. Aston's lips, but what left her body was more than just air. A long, twisted rope of light poured out of her mouth and into Seth's. He took another breath, and Dr. Aston stopped struggling. Fine lines appeared around her eyes and at the corners of her mouth. Another breath, and streaks of white appeared in her auburn hair.

She turned her head slowly and looked at Talli. Her face was twenty years older, maybe thirty, but her eyes were still young, bright, and alive with fear. Another breath, and those eyes rolled back to show whites that in another breath turned yellow. Her skin grew tight and leathery. The soft green dress collapsed around a figure that was quickly becoming nothing more than skin and bones.

Another breath. And another. The thing in Seth's grip was no more than a skeleton. Flecks of parchment skin flaked away from the bony face. The snow-white hair fell off all at once, like a wig slipping from a mannequin. The strand of light pouring from the lipless mouth tapered to a thin string, then a pale thread, and then it was gone.

Seth dropped his bony bundle and turned to Talli. The glow around his body was as bright as the summer sun. "Open wide," he said.

The force of the energy as it struck Talli was as far beyond what he'd given her before as raging fire was beyond a kitchen match. It didn't only burn through her bones, it consumed her flesh.

She could feel every part of her body being remade in the flames of Seth's power. Eventually, the blaze welled up in her mind, and the part of her that was still horrified by Seth—the part that still hoped she could be saved—went screaming into the furnace.

When it was over, Talli looked down and saw a green dress on the floor. "It's pretty," she said.

"Do you like it?" Seth asked. He plucked the dress from the carpet and handed it to her. "Take it with you. It will go beautifully with your eyes."

Something else glittered among the gray and brown fragments that were scattered all over the floor—a necklace. Talli bent to pick it up.

Seth held her back. "No, no, my dear. That's silver." He shook his head. "Very nasty."

He turned Talli toward the door and led her back through the office. She had to step carefully to get over the body in the outer room. With the green dress crushed in her hands, she followed Seth into the night.

Eleven

❧

Thursday

At midnight Chris decided he couldn't take it anymore. "Donna?" he called as he rapped on her bedroom door. "Donna, you up?"

"No," she said. "I'm asleep, and you should be, too."

He knocked on the door again. "Donna, I'm worried about Talli."

There was some soft grumbling from inside, and a few seconds later the door opened. Donna stood there yawning and rubbing her brown eyes. She had always been small. In a huge pink nightshirt, with her short hair all sticking up, she looked about ten years old. "What's wrong with Talli?" she asked around a yawn.

"She was supposed to meet me tonight," Chris said. "I thought maybe she was running late, but now it's been hours. Something's happened, I know it."

"Maybe she got in trouble with her parents," Donna suggested. "Didn't you say her father didn't want her seeing you?"

"I thought about that, too," Chris replied. "But I just walked down to Talli's house and looked. She's still not home."

"So what do you think happened to her?" Donna asked.

Chris grimaced. "Well . . ."

Donna narrowed her eyes. "You're doing it again."

"Doing what?"

"Trying to hide something from your big sister." She took Chris's hand and towed him down the stairs. "Come on. We're going to sit down and drink hot chocolate, and you're going to tell me what's really going on."

Five minutes later they were at the kitchen table with warm mugs in their hands. Chris took a swallow of his steaming hot drink. "There are more vampires in town," he said quickly.

"More?" Donna said. "How many more?"

"Just two."

"Just? Just?" Donna shook her head. "Two cans of soda is *just* two. Two vampires is a lot."

Chris shrugged. "Anyway, I think one of the vampires is after Talli."

136

"How long have you known about these other vampires?" Donna asked.

"Since Monday," Chris replied.

"So why didn't you tell me about it?" Donna asked.

"You know," he said. "You were so worried about the police, and the lies, and so shaken up about Casey. I guess I just didn't want to worry you any more."

"Did you think I was going to break down?"

"Well, yeah, I guess."

Donna set her mug down with a thump. "When have I ever let you down?" she asked.

"Never," Chris said. "But I was afraid it might be too much for you."

"You'll pardon me if I'd prefer to know when there are vampires in town," she said. "I might get really serious about that garlic necklace."

The doorbell rang. Chris felt a flash of fear run through him as he turned and looked at the door. "It's Them," he said.

"You don't know that," Donna told him shakily. "Maybe it's Talli." She looked down at herself. "Whoever it is, I'm not dressed to go to the door."

Chris glanced at the raggedy T-shirt and gym shorts he was wearing. "I'm not either," he said. The doorbell rang again, followed by a loud pounding on the door.

"Somebody better answer it," Donna said. She walked across the kitchen and opened a

137

cabinet. Inside was a dark cherrywood box. She flipped open the top and brought out a knife of gleaming sterling sliver.

"I'll do it," Chris said. He took the knife from his sister's hand.

"Don't try to be a knight in shining armor," she said.

"I'm not," he said. "But I know more about what's going on than you do. This is something that I should do."

With Donna following, Chris went into the living room and approached the door. He gripped the knife tightly in his right hand and pulled the door open with his left.

Officer Lansky stood on the doorstep with his hands shoved down into the pockets of his wool coat. He looked Chris up and down. "You always come to the door with a knife, Delany?" he asked.

"I do when someone knocks at this time of night," Chris said.

"Sorry if I disturbed your beauty sleep," Lansky said sarcastically. "We want to talk to you."

"We who?"

Another figure stepped out of the shadows. Chris tensed, but relaxed when he saw that it was Talli's father.

"We're looking for Talli," Jake McAlister said. "Do you know where she is, Chris?"

Chris shook his head. "No, I haven't seen her."

Talli's father nodded. "All right. Come on, Lansky, let's go."

"I'm not done talking to this one," Lansky said. He jerked his head toward the living room. "You going to let me in?"

Chris started to step back, but Donna came rushing up and blocked Lansky's entry. "Get back," she said. "No one's coming in here tonight."

Lansky stepped back in surprise. Donna stood with her hands planted on her hips. Somehow, small as she was, standing barefoot in front of the open door with a pink gown flapping around her knees, Donna still managed to look intimidating. "If you want to talk to us," she said. "You come back and do it at a decent hour."

"I can get a warrant, if that's what you want," Lansky said. Chris could see that Lansky's face had turned beet-red. He couldn't tell if it was from anger or embarrassment.

Jake McAlister stepped up and spoke to the fuming police officer. "We've got no reason to go in there," he said. "If we wake up Judge Wyodak at this hour and ask him for a warrant, he'll have us both locked up."

Lansky turned on him with an expression that was almost a snarl. "It's your daughter who's missing," he said. "Don't you want to find her?"

The muscles tightened along McAlister's broad jaw. "Talli is my daughter," he said. "And I trust her judgment." He looked up the steps at Chris. "She says this boy is her friend, and that's good enough for me. Come on, Lansky. She's not here." He turned and walked back to the squad car parked at the curb.

Lansky watched him go. "Idiot," he said under his breath, but loud enough for Chris to hear. The skinny police officer turned back to the house. "You can bet that I'll be wanting to talk to both of you." Then he turned and stomped through the snow to the car.

Donna closed the door and leaned against it. "Thank goodness," she said.

"I don't understand," Chris said. "Why didn't you let Lansky come in? For once we really don't have anything to hide."

"Two reasons," replied his sister. "First, I didn't want him coming in here when I'm not dressed. Second, don't you remember one of the rules that we learned at the library, you fierce vampire hunter?"

Chris shook his head. "Sorry, you lost me."

"It was one of the few that were real," Donna said. "Vampires have trouble coming into your house unless you invite them." She patted Chris on the shoulder as she went past him and started up the stairs.

"You don't think Lansky's a vampire, do you?" Chris called after her.

"Right now," she said without turning her head, "I think everyone's a vampire—you said they can look however they want. I'm going back to sleep. School starts in a few hours. If we're going to be attacked by vampires, I want to at least be rested." She went into her bedroom and closed the door.

Chris thought about going to sleep, but he didn't think about it too hard. Talli was out there somewhere, and he had a good idea whom she was with. He walked across the cold wooden floor and pushed aside the curtains. Westerberg was a small town, and it was darker outside than Chicago had ever been. A few flakes of snow fell slowly from the blackness overhead, spiraling down in the absolutely still air.

He wondered where Sky was. If the things she'd told him were true, then Talli was in the worst kind of danger. On the other hand, maybe everything Sky had said was a lie.

Chris clenched his fists in frustration. For all he knew, Seth could be getting ready to leave Westerberg and take Talli with him. Chris wanted to throw on some clothes and charge out into the night. But the night was Seth's world, not his. He knew from experience that vampires were much more powerful in the darkness. That was another one of the true legends. If Chris went out there now, alone and without a plan, Seth would probably take his head off. He let the curtains slide back over the w and went into the kitchen.

The pot they'd used to boil wat

late was still on the stove. Chris filled it with water and sat down at the table to wait. Somewhere out there Talli was in trouble, and he knew there was nothing he could do about it. He sipped at the cold dregs of his chocolate and wondered how long it was before dawn. The next thing he knew, Donna was shaking him awake.

"Better get up if you want to go to school," she said.

Chris rubbed his eyes and looked at the kitchen window. It wasn't really dark anymore, but the sky was nothing but a gray blur. "What time is it?" he asked.

Donna looked at her watch. "It's almost seven," she said. "I'm late because the power went out. There was quite a bit of snow last night."

Still groggy from sleep, Chris went over to the window and looked out. What looked like a fresh foot of snow lay on top of the blanket that had already covered the ground. All the footprints and tire tracks had been erased by the fresh fall. "Are they even going to have school today?" he asked. "It looks pretty bad out there."

Donna opened the refrigerator and pushed things around inside. "They probably wouldn't, but there's been so much snow this year that we'll be going to school through most of June." She came out with an apple and closed the door.

"I think they'd have school now even if we had a blizzard."

"I don't think I'm going," Chris said. "I can't just go on like nothing's happened. Talli's missing. I need to stay here and come up with some way to help her."

"It's going to get awfully chilly in this place," his sister said. "The power's still out, and the heat's electric."

"I can throw a couple of logs in the fireplace," he said. "Besides, I'm hoping I won't be in here all day."

Donna put the apple down on the counter and walked over to him. "Listen, this has always been serious, but now it's deadly. Talli's gone, Chris. For all you know, she went with them willingly. If she comes back, that'll be great, but I don't want you running off to try and save her."

"I have to."

"No, you don't. What you've got to do is take care of yourself." She sighed. "I don't want to sound cold. I know you like Talli. I like her, too. I'd take a lot of chances if I thought it would help her. But I don't want you throwing your life away. Understand?" She picked up the apple and took a large bite. "I'm going on to school," she said after she swallowed. "You coming?"

Chris shook his head. "No. I'll stay here in case Talli decides to call. Let me know if she shows up at school, okay?"

"Promise me you won't leave the house," said his sister.

"I promise I'll be careful," he replied.

Donna scowled at him. "That's not the same thing, but you better at least keep that promise." She picked up her purse and headed for the front door. A second later she was back in the kitchen. "Keys?" she asked.

Chris grinned. It was nice that some things didn't change. "On the table by the front door," he said.

Donna nodded and headed out. Chris stood by the window and watched her back slowly out of the driveway and fishtail her way up the snowy street; then he went back to the table and sat down.

He needed a plan. Westerberg might be a small town, but it was way too big to start knocking on doors looking for Talli. He had no idea where to go. When Alex had come back, he'd been drawn to Volker's old house. If the house were still standing, Chris would have investigated it right away. But Volker's house was nothing but a pile of ashes and a hole in the ground. Chris didn't think the dapper Seth would be hanging out in a place like that.

He was startled out of his thoughts by the doorbell. Wishing that he had taken the time to get dressed, he padded into the living room and opened the door. He expected it to be Lansky coming back for the promised visit, but instead a middle-aged man in dull-gray coveralls stood there.

"Can I help you?" Chris asked.

"Yeah," said the man. "It's the power. I need to come inside and check your meter before I turn the power back on."

"I don't know . . . ," Chris started.

"Hey, pal," the man said, "it's no skin off my nose, but if you don't let me in, the whole block will be in the dark."

Chris thought for a second, then nodded. "All right, come on in."

"Thanks, pal." The man stepped past Chris, then turned to him with a wide grin. "You were so easy," he said. "Check your meter. I can't believe you fell for that." The man's features began to flow and change.

Chris looked around madly, trying to spot the silver knife he'd been carrying the night before. "Stay back," he warned.

The repair man's face grew smooth and heart-shaped, and the form within the coveralls grew much more slender. "Relax," Sky said. "It's me."

Chris fell back against the wall and put his hand to his chest to make sure his heart was still beating. "Why the heck did you do that?" he asked.

"Just testing you," Sky said. "You failed."

"Is Talli okay?" Chris asked. "Where is she?"

"She's with Seth." Sky unzipped the coveralls

to reveal a short-sleeved black T-shirt and jeans. She tossed the coveralls on a chair and flopped down on the couch. "I spent most of the night cleaning up the party they had at her psychiatrist's office, so Seth was free to spend time with his new little toy."

"What happened at the psychiatrist's office? Did the psychiatrist see anything?"

Sky drew a finger across her throat. "Dead as you can get. The receptionist, too. You better hope no more vampires settle in this town. Otherwise, they're going to have to change the population signs."

Chris bit his lip. "How could Talli watch her doctor be killed and still go with Seth? Did she go with him on purpose? I mean, is it what she wanted?"

"She doesn't want anything right now," Sky said with a shrug. "She's turned, Chris. She's true gold, as Seth would say. Right now her brain's working about as well as a spoon with a hole in it. She'll do whatever Seth says. It'll take her a bit before she starts the gears turning on her own again."

Chris eased the front door closed and sat down on the chair across from Sky. "When her mind comes back, will she remember everything? Will she be the same as she was?"

"Hard to say," Sky said. "She'll be zombified for a few hours, or maybe a few days. After that she might be ready to run for home." She put her long legs up on the coffee table and arched her back as she stretched. "On the other hand, she might want to come home and bite the heads off of dear old Mom and Dad. It happens."

"So what do we do?" Chris asked. "We've got to help her."

"Before we do anything," Sky said, "you've got to do something for me."

"What?"

"Tell me how you're going to turn me back."

"Can't it wait?" Chris asked. "At least until we get Talli away from him."

Sky shook her head. "He suspects me. Seth knows I'm up to something. Right now he's too taken with your sweet little Talli to pay much attention, but any minute now he's going to look up and squash us both." She smiled sweetly. "Frankly, just in case he makes jam out of you, I want the secret now."

"Well, in a way, that makes what I'm going to say easier," Chris said. He tried to smile, but the muscles in his face seemed to be numb. "I think I do have a way to turn vampires back."

"And it is?"

"We have to kill Seth."

Sky sucked in a deep breath and leaned back on the couch. "We're dead meat," she said.

Twelve

"Wake up, dear," Seth said. "We need to get some work done."

Talli opened her eyes. It was light outside, and that hurt. She struggled to find the word. "Rest," she managed at last. "Need rest."

"You're talking already," Seth said. "That's excellent progress." He reached down and took her hand. "I know you don't feel like getting out just now, but we have to do a few errands today if we're going to be ready to leave this town tonight."

Talli was able to understand only about half his words. Her brain seemed to have been packed away in cotton, and every thought was an effort. There was only one thing she could think of that she wanted as much as she wanted rest. "Food?" she asked.

"Not right now," Seth said, "but perhaps there will be time later. Come along."

He pulled her up from the bed and led her down a hallway to a living room cluttered with dusty furniture and long racks of trophies. Heavy curtains blocked the light from the windows and kept the room filled with shadows. A figure sat at the far end of the room, a gaunt man whose eyes didn't move as Seth and Talli walked toward him.

"Good afternoon, Mr. Pays," Seth said to him. "Are you ready?"

"I'm always ready, Coach," mumbled the man.

"That's fine, Mr. Pays. Come along with us, will you?"

The man rose stiffly to his feet and walked alongside them. Talli thought he looked familiar, but she wasn't sure. She hissed as Seth opened the front door and let in the cold gray winter light.

"Don't worry," he said. "You've got too much energy for it to hurt you."

Talli blinked at the light. It didn't hurt, but she was afraid of it anyway. She wanted to go back into the shadows, where it was safe, but Seth pulled her out into the day. He led her around the house, Pays still staggering along at their side. There was an old wooden garage behind the house, with a tangle of brown vines clinging to the walls, and a roof that sagged

150

under the weight of the snow. Seth pulled his hand free of Talli's and swung open the rickety door at the front of the garage. There was an orange car inside. Like the gaunt man, the car seemed familiar.

"Get in the car," Seth said. Talli started for the driver's side, but Seth took her arm and steered her around to the passenger side. "I'm afraid you're in no condition to drive at the moment," he said. He had her climb into the backseat and let the tall man perch in front. Then Seth got behind the wheel, started the car, and drove it out onto the icy street.

For Talli everything blurred together as they drove. House after house went past, and for almost every one of them, some vague memory stirred inside her. But before she could put any of these pieces together, the house was past and she was dealing with the next puzzle piece. After a while she closed her eyes and rested from the dizzying flurry of images.

After a few moments with her eyes shut, she slipped back into the dark sleep. She opened her eyes again only when the car door slammed. She looked up and saw that the tall man had climbed out of the car and was walking away down the sidewalk. Talli tried to shake some of the cobwebs out of her head. "Where?" she asked.

Seth glanced back at her and smiled. "You're awake. Good. Why don't you come sit in the front? I want you to be seen."

Still groggy, Talli climbed out of the backseat and slumped down in the front. She tried to find the words to ask her question. "The man," she said. "Where . . . ?"

"Ah, the coach," Seth said. "Our friend Mr. Pays has been waiting for days to perform an errand for me, and now I've given him permission." He chuckled softly. "I believe Mr. Pays is a very happy man."

Talli frowned at the thin form of Coach Pays walking away in the snow. "Happy?" she said.

"Yes," Seth said. He took his hands from the wheel and sat up very straight. "Now, if you'll excuse me, it's time to make some changes." Seth's hair lightened to a pale brown and grew curly. His features softened and his chin grew a bit rounder. He turned to her with a new face. "How do I look?" he asked.

Talli knew that face. "Chris," she said.

"That's right," he said, inspecting himself in the rearview mirror. "Chris Delany. Now, let's go make sure that the local authorities know just who to blame for all their problems."

He drove the car up the hill and through the middle of downtown Westerberg. Only a few people were out on the streets, and most of the sidewalks hadn't yet been cleaned. Talli kept glancing over at Seth as he drove. She had remembered the name that went with the face he was wearing, but she knew there was more that she was forgetting.

He turned into the street alongside the courthouse and stopped at the town's one traffic light. Seth pursed his lips and drummed his fingers on the steering wheel. "Hmmm. We've got to find just the right way to make our little announcement."

"Announcement," Talli repeated.

"That's right," Seth said. He continued to stare for a moment, then said, "Oh, well. Let's just try the direct approach, why don't we? Where's the police station in this poor excuse for a town?"

He had to ask the question twice more before Talli understood and was able to point him in the right direction. A few minutes later they pulled up to the curb across the street from a brick building surrounded by parked police cars.

"We could go inside," Seth said, "but that might lead to complications." He turned his wrist and glanced at his watch. "We've plenty of time. Let's just wait until someone comes out."

Talli was almost asleep again when Seth spoke up. "There," he said. "That looks like a fine upstanding example of Westerberg's police force. Do you recognize that officer, dear?"

Talli turned her head and saw a large man moving down the row of parked cars. He was some distance away, but he seemed to be looking at the car where Talli was sitting. Suddenly he smiled and began to walk rapidly toward them. She knew who the man was, but it took her several seconds to put that thought in words. "That's my father," she said.

"Your father? How wonderful," said Seth. "How absolutely perfect. Now, I want you to open your car door. Open it, but do not get out, understand?"

Talli nodded. She clawed clumsily at the door handle, got a grip on it, and pushed the door open. In the side mirror she saw her father stepping over a bank of plowed snow. He was only about fifty feet away.

"Now scream," Seth said.

Talli stared at him. "Scream?" she asked.

"Scream!" Seth shouted.

Talli screamed. She forced the air from her lungs in a long, tearing rush that would have made any of the actors in the horror movies she used to watch quite proud.

"Very good," Seth said calmly. He leaned across her and pulled the door shut, then slammed on the gas. The wheels spun wildly as the car moved away from the curb and fishtailed down the street.

In the mirror Talli saw her father running down the slick road. The car threw a wave of dirty half-frozen slush in his face, but he kept coming. He was gaining on them with each long step. He was ten feet away. Five.

Then the tires hit a patch of clean pavement

and the car leaped ahead. Talli's father made a diving grab for the car, missed, and fell face-down in the street. He was up in only a moment. He turned and ran back toward the police station.

"We only have a few minutes to go before they're after us in the patrol cars," Seth said. "I'm quite a skilled driver, but they will have an advantage over me in knowledge of the local roads. The prudent thing for us to do is to vacate this vehicle and proceed on foot."

"Ditch the car," Talli said.

"Yes," Seth replied. He looked over at her and gave her another of his bright smiles. "I believe you're feeling better."

She was. The scream had been the sound of madness, but somehow making that noise had helped clear some of the fog from Talli's mind. She couldn't remember how she had gotten here, or what was going on, but she understood they had to get rid of the car before the police caught up with them.

Seth steered the car around a sharp corner. For a moment two wheels left the road. There was a tearing squeal as the door beside Talli rubbed against a metal guardrail. She looked over and down to the icy river thirty feet below. Then Seth pulled the car out of its slide and they went rocketing down a straight slope until they came to the next curve. This time the car spun all the way around before pointing its nose back along the road.

Seth laughed. "Isn't this fun, Talli?"

"It's scary," she said.

"There's no need for you to be afraid," he assured her. "Even if we were to crash into a brick wall, I've given you enough energy to rebuild yourself ten times over. Rejoice in your power! Revel in it. We have the freedom to behave as we want without concern for being injured. It's a freedom the pitiful greens will never know."

Despite his words Talli still felt fear. It might be true that she could survive a wreck, but it didn't sound very appealing. She turned her mind to figuring out where they could leave the car.

Somewhere behind them a police siren sounded. Seth's smile turned to a frown, and he brought the car to a stop at the next intersection. "All good things must come to an end," he said. "And as fun as this little motor chase could be, we can't afford to become too entangled with the local authorities."

"School," Talli said.

"What's that?"

"We can leave the car at the school," she said.

"Oh, that's good," Seth said. "There's probably not a larger group of cars to be found in this tiny town, so we should have no problem hiding. And when we prepare to leave, we'll have our choice of vehicle. Very good. You really are thinking much more clearly, aren't you?"

Talli smiled, pleased with his compliment. "Thank you," she said.

"Now," Seth said, "if you can direct me to this school before the police catch up with us, we'll be in fine shape."

Talli showed him which way to turn, and a few minutes later he guided the car into the parking lot of Westerberg High. The harsh winter had eaten a thousand potholes in the poorly maintained parking lot. Talli's head brushed the ceiling of the car several times as Seth drove though the ruts and over speed bumps at a bonejarring pace. He selected a slot between a minivan and a pickup. The spot was so narrow that no student had dared to park in it. Seth managed expertly, bringing Talli's old orange Pinto into the place with scarcely two inches of space on either side.

They had barely stopped before a police car turned off the main highway and went cruising down the road beside the school. It slowed as it passed the parking lot, and Talli thought she could see the officers inside looking their way. Then the police car sped up and disappeared over the nearest hill. "And there we are," Seth said. "A perfect escape, and accomplished with the minimum of effort thanks to your timely suggestion."

Talli looked out at the school building. More memories were floating up to the surface of her confused mind. She saw images of what had happened, but she couldn't put them together to form any kind of complete picture. She remembered Volker, and how he had killed her friends. Volker had been a vampire. But Talli was a vampire, too. So why had he hurt her? Why had she been forced to kill him? Then Alex had come back, and he had died, too. Now Seth had come. He'd said he would help her, and he was still here, taking care of her.

Bad people were trying to hurt Seth. Trying to hurt her, too. Talli didn't understand why, but she was determined that they wouldn't take Seth away from her the way that Alex had been taken away.

Seth looked at his watch again. "Sky is arranging a flight from the nearest airport and taking care of our other travel plans today. We're to meet her at nightfall, and it's likely that she won't be back till then." He followed Talli's gaze to the school, and a smile slowly grew on his face. "This is the same school that you attend?" he asked.

Talli nodded. "I go here."

"And Chris Delany attends this school as well?"

Images came to Talli. Chris in the school cafeteria, his face—the same face now worn by Seth—smiling at her from across a table. She nodded. "This is his school."

"What a happy coincidence," Seth said. He

looked out his window. "I don't believe that even I can make it out the door. We'll have to pop the hatch to escape. Then we'll pay a visit to your school." He turned to her with the broadest smile she had seen yet. "We still have time for one last amusement before we leave this place," he said. "One last little present for your friend Chris."

Coach Pays had tried to cut straight through the woods to reach his goal. He hadn't used the shortcut in years, and with all the snow covering up the paths, he had gotten lost. He worried that he would never find his way out, and then his job would never be finished; but he finally found the road.

The wonderful feeling inside him came back. Soon he would take care of the person that had hurt his Casey. He reached the house where the boy lived and felt in his pants pocket for the gun. It was gone.

He plunged his hand in and pulled the lining inside out. He made a soft cry at his loss. He had been an idiot. A fool. The gun was probably somewhere back in the woods, lost in a snow-drift. Then he felt the comforting lump against his side. It was in his coat pocket.

He reached in and pulled out the gun, laughing at himself as he did so. The gun was cold and beautiful. Coach Pays was a practiced shooter. He pulled out the clip and checked to make sure it was full. Then he shoved it back in, put his palm on the top of the gun, and pushed back the action to load the first shell. "Eight in the clip, and one in the chamber," he whispered. "That should be more than enough for one boy."

In fact, the gun was a nine-millimeter, and nine bullets from it were more than enough for a whole roomful of boys. But Coach Pays wasn't worried about saving bullets. He meant to use every shot.

Thirteen

"Garlic?" Chris asked.

"That mostly bothers the new ones," Sky replied. "When you're first turned, you don't have a lot of control over your senses." She picked up the clove of garlic from the tray that Chris had brought in, sniffed it, and wrinkled her nose. "Sight and smell and taste are all different for us. The smell would probably be strong enough right now to send Talli running. It still bothers me a little bit. Seth could probably walk through a warehouse of the stuff without a problem."

"Holy water?" Chris asked.

"Nope," Sky said. "Nothing to it. Salt water's kind of bad. It stings if it gets on you, and lots of golds don't like to travel over the ocean. But I don't think it would seriously hurt me even if you dumped a whole bucket of the stuff over my head."

"Well, I wouldn't know where to get holy water by the gallon, anyway," Chris said. "How about crosses?"

"If they're made out of silver, then it hurts to touch them. Otherwise, it's tough luck for the guy waving the cross." She picked up a small wooden cross that Chris had put on the table and twirled it around in her fingers. "See? Nothing."

"Any other kind of religious symbols do anything?" he asked, but without much hope.

"Not that I know of," she said with a shrug. "If you can think of anything I haven't seen, I'm willing to try it, but I think we'd be wasting our time."

Chris sighed. "There was so much religious stuff in all the old books, I was hoping there'd be something to it."

"Well, churches are a problem," Sky said. "Most public buildings we can come and go as we want, but churches are even harder to get into than houses. Every time I get near one, it's like I feel something pushing me away."

"That's great, but I don't see how we can use that as a weapon." Chris looked down at the collection of things on the table. "Anything I forgot to ask about?"

"Fire works really well," Sky said. "I think golds are burned easier than regular people. And don't forget that we can be hurt by most of the same things that hurt everybody else: car wrecks, falls, little pieces of lead flying through our bodies at high speed . . ."

"You mean I could just shoot Seth?"

"You could, and he'd be hurt for a while, but he'd heal really fast," she said. "I said we could be hurt by that, not killed. If you actually want to kill him, you'd have to do some really major damage."

"Like what?" Chris asked.

She thought for a second. "Dropping a safe on him would probably do it, but it'd be hard to arrange. You'd have to pretty well make jelly out of him if you want to keep him from getting up again."

"Like you said, that doesn't sound too easy to arrange." Chris frowned down at the table, then reached out and picked up the knife. "So it really comes down to this," he said.

Sky leaned away from him. "Be careful with that," she said. "Just a nick from it could kill me."

"Would it kill Seth, too?" Chris asked.

She shrugged. "Silver's like an allergy. Some golds can take being stabbed with that knife and keep on going. Others would fall over dead if they just touched it. I've managed to stay away from the stuff myself, so I don't know how sensitive I am."

Chris fingered the edge of the blade. "You

163

know, there's something I thought of earlier. Silver's a good conductor. Now you say that salt water gives you problems, too. How about—"

He was interrupted by the ringing of the doorbell. "Great," he said. "Now who is it?" He started to go to the door.

"Wait," Sky warned. "It could be Seth."

Chris looked at her and frowned. "Why would he come here?"

"He wants to get rid of you," she said. "Seth's a big one for never leaving any witnesses." She tossed the cross back onto the table and sent the garlic clove flying with a flick of her finger. "Besides, he knows that you killed Volker. Not killing a gold is about the only rule Seth lives by. He'll make sure you die for that."

Chris opened his mouth to say that he hadn't killed Volker, that Talli had done it, but Talli was in enough danger without anyone knowing that. "Thanks for telling me," Chris said. The bell sounded again. "So do I answer the door or not?"

"Answer it," she said, "but this time try not to invite anyone in."

"Got it." Chris walked to the door and pulled it open. Officer Lansky stood there, with Jake McAlister close behind. "Back for more questioning?" Chris asked.

Without warning Lansky put a hand on Chris's chest and shoved him back into the house. "No questions this time, sport," he snarled. Before Chris could recover his balance, Lansky grabbed him by the arm and spun him around. "Drop the knife!" he shouted.

Chris opened his hand and let the knife fall to the floor. "What's—"

Lansky shoved him against the door and pulled his hands behind his back. "We're going to have plenty of time to talk," he said. "Because you're under arrest."

"For what?" Chris asked. He winced as Lansky pushed his arms up and clamped handcuffs around his wrists. "I didn't do anything!"

Lansky whirled him around. "How about kidnapping, huh? How about grand theft auto?"

Jake McAlister pushed Lansky aside and put his broad face very close to Chris's. "Where is she?" he asked. "What have you done with her?"

"You mean Talli?" Chris asked.

From the steps Lansky snorted. "Of course he means Talli, you son of a—"

"Quiet," McAlister said. His dark eyes were locked on Chris's face. "Just tell me where she is, Chris. Tell me now."

Chris shook his head. "I don't know," he said.

"I saw you with her not twenty minutes ago," McAlister said. "Where is she?"

"It wasn't me. I've been here all day. Just ask . . ." Chris turned his head toward the couch where Sky had been sitting. She was gone.

"Just ask who?"

Chris stared at the empty couch. "Nobody," he said.

McAlister stood still for a moment; then he nodded slowly. "Take him downtown," he said to Lansky. "I'm going to stay here and search the place. Call me if he says anything." He stepped back. "Oh," he added, "be sure to read him his rights. I don't want any slipups on this one."

Lansky stepped past Talli's father and gripped Chris by the shoulder. "There won't be any slipups," he said. "I'll make this punk talk. Then next time maybe you'll listen to me in the first place."

He pushed Chris out of the house and hustled him into the backseat of the waiting patrol car. When the door was shut, Chris noticed that there were no handles on the inside. With his hands cuffed behind his back, he probably wouldn't have been able to do anything about it anyway. A wire screen separated him from where Lansky sat in the front seat. "Better think up a story now, kid," the skinny police officer said over his shoulder. "And it better be a good one." He reached over his head and flipped a switch that started the sirens howling.

Chris leaned back against the cold vinyl seat. If Talli had been seen, then at least she was still alive. Her father said he had seen Chris with her. There was little doubt what that meant: Seth was masquerading as him.

166

Probably to cause me just this kind of trouble, he thought. Chris only hoped that it didn't go any further. The thought of Seth doing something really horrible while wearing his face was one of the most awful things he could think of.

Lansky pulled the car right up to the steps of the police station and led Chris inside. He was marched through the squad room, where a half-dozen police officers stopped to watch him pass. In a town the size of Westerberg, major crimes were pretty rare. Or at least they had been before Volker came to town. With all those unsolved disappearances, Chris wasn't surprised that every officer on the squad seemed anxious to put him away. Just being accused of kidnapping a teenage girl in a town like Westerberg was probably enough to start people itching to punch his lights out. With a police officer's daughter involved, Chris was thankful to make it through the station without being shot.

He stood in front of a poster and held up an arrest-record number as his picture was taken from the front and from the side. Then he sat down and let his hands be smeared with black ink so he could roll his fingerprints onto a card.

"Have a fax of these sent up to Chicago," Lansky told the officer who took the prints. "There might be something in their files that matches."

Chris thought about saying something, but he was too worried even to be mad. Talli was out there with Seth. He didn't have time to think about trading insults with Lansky; he only had to convince them to let him go so he could do something.

Ten minutes after coming into the station, Chris was back in the small gray room where they had held him a few days before. Lansky was again leaning against the wall with his cigarette in hand. It was if the last three days hadn't happened. Except that they had, and things were ten times worse than when Chris had been in this room before.

"You ready to tell us where you put Talli McAlister?" Lansky asked.

"I haven't seen Talli since the day before yesterday," Chris said.

Lansky blew out a long stream of blue-white smoke. "Okay. So how about telling us where you stashed the car?"

"What car?"

The lighted cigarette flew across the room and bounced on the table in front of Chris. "I'm not going to screw around with you, kid," Lansky said. "I hear you drove out of here pretty fast. For all I know, you wrecked that girl's car in the snow somewhere and left her to freeze. Maybe you even drove the car into the river."

He stepped across the room with two quick strides and slammed his fists down on the table. The smoldering cigarette bounced and rolled onto the floor. "You tell me where she is," Lansky screamed into Chris's face. "You tell me now!"

Chris leaned away from him, blinking against the smoke. "I told you, I don't know where she is. I wish I did, but I don't."

Lansky looked as if he wanted to spit. A vein bulged out in the center of his forehead, and his lips curled back from his nicotine-yellowed teeth as he prepared to launch his next attack. The door opened, and a young officer looked in. Lansky whirled on her. "What is it?"

"You need to come out here for a second," the police officer said.

"Not now," Lansky replied. "I'm just getting started."

"It's important."

Lansky scowled. "It better be." He followed the young officer out of the room, and the door slammed shut.

Chris put his elbows up on the table and rested his head on his hands. A few seconds later the door opened again. "I don't know where she is," he said tiredly.

"I know that," said a woman's voice.

Chris looked up to see his sister Donna standing inside the door with a uniformed officer right behind her. "When did you get here?" he asked.

Donna turned to the officer. "If you'll leave us alone for just a few minutes?"

169

"Sure," the man said. He stepped back and closed the door.

Chris stood up and walked over to his sister. "I'm sorry," he said. "It must have been embarrassing to be dragged out of school in front of everyone."

She looked up at him with an unexpected grin. "That's okay," she said. "I didn't go to school today."

"But I saw you leave."

She shook her head. "Nope, not me. I watched the policemen take you away. Sorry I didn't hang around to help."

Chris blinked and looked at her more closely. "Sky?" he whispered. "Is that you?" Nervously, he glanced at the two-way mirror.

"In the flesh," she replied. "Well, in somebody's flesh, anyway. But I can still see like a vampire, and there aren't any greens on the other side of this mirror. Relax."

Chris shook his head and stepped back to lean against the table. "All this shape-shifting stuff is weird."

"Yeah, well, it's weird for me, too," Sky said. She walked over to the mirrored wall and tugged at her sweater. "Your sister is really, really short. I feel like a Munchkin."

"She's not that short."

"She's short enough," Sky said. She wrinkled her nose at Donna's face in the mirror. "Follow the yellow-brick road," she said in a squeaky voice.

170

"All right, since you're pretending to be my sister," Chris said, "did you bring some pretend bail money to get me out?"

She turned away from her reflection and grinned at him again. "Don't have to."

"Why not?" he asked. Then he held up his hands. "Don't tell me. We're going to break out of jail, right?"

"Nope," she said. "They're going to let you go."

Chris sat down in the chair. "This is moving too fast for me. Why would they let me go?"

The door opened, and Lansky walked in with Talli's father at his shoulder. "We found the car," he said.

"Where?" Chris asked. "Did you find Talli? Is she okay?"

"We haven't found Talli," Jake McAlister said. "The car was in the school parking lot. Any way we figure it, it doesn't seem possible that you could have walked from the school to your house in the time it took us to get there."

He stepped past Lansky and stuck out his big hand. "I'm sorry, Chris," he said. "I thought it was you in Talli's car, but it must have been someone else."

Chris stood and took the offered hand. "I'm worried about Talli, too," he said. "I hope you find whoever has her."

"Thanks," Talli's father said. "You can leave whenever you're ready." He turned and left the room.

Lansky looked Chris up and down. "Don't expect any apology from me, Delany," he said. "I still think you're in this thing up to your neck. And when I find out how, I'm going to push you under." With one last glare he turned and stomped off down the hall.

"Nice guy," Sky said.

"Yeah," Chris said. "So what do we do now?"

"I was supposed to spend today making plane reservations at the airport about sixty miles from here," she said. "I didn't make any reservations. Seth's going to know I've been up to something, so we have to take him out now."

"Do you know where to find them?" Chris asked.

Sky nodded. "They're in the Payses' house."

"Pays? Like Casey Pays? Why are they there?"

"Casey's father was following you around. He thinks you've got his daughter hidden somewhere."

Chris frowned. "He's almost right. Alex turned Casey into a vampire, and I killed her."

"Alex?" Sky asked. "Who's Alex?"

"I'll tell you on the way," Chris replied. "It's a long story."

Willard Pays's knuckles were white as he gripped the steering wheel. He had been seconds away from taking care of the boy when the police had shown up and ruined everything.

172

More frustrating minutes had been spent walking back to his own house and getting his truck. Now the boy was inside the police station. He knew the police would never do what was right. Coach Seth had helped him understand that only death would stop this boy from hurting other young girls like Casey. It was Pays's duty to kill him. Pays would not hide from the police again. If he had to, he would march right into the police station and shoot him there.

His heart jumped as the door to the station opened and the boy came out. They had let him go. "They don't know anything," he said aloud. The boy's sister was with him. Coach Seth hadn't said anything about her, and Pays wouldn't shoot her if he didn't have to, but he wasn't going to let her get in the way of killing the boy.

He watched the pair get into the long black car he had first seen by the cemetery and drive away. Pays checked to see that his pistol was still on the seat beside him, then followed close behind.

Fourteen

Donna looked up as they came into the room. "Chris! You found Talli. That's great."

"Yes. I found her," Seth said. "I think she'll be all right now."

"I'll be all right now," Talli said.

"You mean you're not a half vampire anymore?" Donna asked excitedly.

"That's right," Seth said. "We took care of that little problem."

"That's incredible!" Donna cried. "Now maybe we can finally get on with some kind of normal life."

Seth smiled at her. "Can we have a ride, sis? Talli's car isn't working."

"I have to do drama club before I can leave," Donna said. "I was getting ready to head over there when you guys came in. If you can wait, I'll give you a ride after."

Seth put an arm around Talli's shoulders. "We'll be happy to wait," he said.

Donna gave him a slightly puzzled look. "Okay. Come on into the auditorium with me. It ought to be a short meeting today."

Talli was the last one into the auditorium. It was such a wonderful place, so dark and cool and comfortable. She thought she could remember not liking this place, but she couldn't remember why. She let Seth steer her to a spot in the back row, far behind and above the students who milled about near the stage.

"Look at all the energy," Seth whispered.

In the dim light of the auditorium, the green glow that surrounded all the people was visible. Hunger awakened in Talli as she watched them laughing and talking. "Will we feed?" she asked.

"Of course," Seth said. "We'll feed from the best." He pointed over the rows of seats.

Standing in front of the students, Donna glowed brighter than all the others. Talli remembered that she had always been impressed by Donna's energy and enthusiasm. Now she could see that energy—a green fire that followed the young teacher as she hurried back and forth. She looked twice as bright as anyone else in the room. Talli's hunger surged at the thought, but something else stirred inside her as well. A feeling that made her uneasy. "Do we have to feed from Donna?" she asked.

176

"Look at her," Seth said. "She's a wonder. We could sip energy from her for a week and still be more than satisfied. If we were to drain her fully, as I did the late Dr. Aston, we would have more power than we could handle." There was obvious emotion in his voice, and Talli saw threads of red desire looping through the colors that surrounded him.

"Couldn't we use someone else?" she asked.

He turned to her with one eyebrow raised and his lips twisted in a smirk—an expression that looked strange on Chris's features. "What is this?" he asked. "Sympathy? When you were a green, you had little thought for the cattle that served to feed you. Now you're above these greens the way you used to be above the cattle. You're a wolf among the sheep, Talli. Save your feelings for others like yourself, don't waste it on your supper."

"But Donna was my friend," Talli said.

"'Was' is the important word there," he said. "She was your friend. You can have no friends among the greens now, only enemies and food."

Talli sorted through the jumble of names and images in her mind. "What about Chris?" she asked.

Seth chuckled softly. "You don't have to worry about Chris anymore. Chris is no longer a problem."

She felt confused. A few minutes before, feeding and pleasing Seth had been all she

177

wanted. Now things were getting muddled.

Students began to file out of the auditorium. They laughed and chatted as they went past. A few of them waved or stopped to say hello to Talli. She wanted to get out of her seat and join them. If she could join in that laughing crowd, she could forget all about Seth and be a normal person again. Then the image of Dr. Aston crumbling into dust came to her. Talli slumped back in her chair. Seth was right—she could never be a regular person again.

"Come along," Seth said after the last student had passed. "Let's go collect my sweet sister."

Donna was still shoving papers into her bag when they reached the bottom of the sloping aisle. She looked up at them and smiled. "We didn't get much accomplished today," she said. "Grant Winchell is supposed to be the director for the upcoming play, and he's been sick for the last couple of days. One of the other teachers tells me they found him unconscious out in the snow, and now he's very ill. I hate to do it, but if he doesn't get better soon, I'm going to have to ask his assistant to take over."

"I think Grant will be better in another day or so," Seth said.

"You know something about it?" Donna asked.

Seth held up his hands. "Just a hunch."

"I guess we can go now." Donna picked up

her bag, then tilted her head and looked at Seth. "Where'd you get that sweater?"

He shrugged. "Something old."

"I don't remember it," Donna said.

"Well, I wouldn't expect you to remember my entire wardrobe."

Donna's face became very still. "I don't forget clothes. What do I always forget, Chris?" she asked.

"Faces?"

Donna backed away and shook her head slowly. "The car keys."

"That's right," Seth said. "You forget the car keys."

Donna dropped her bag to the floor. "You're not Chris."

Seth slapped a hand to his chest and put on an expression of exaggerated pain. "How can you say that?"

Donna's small hands bunched into fists. "Have you hurt my brother?" she demanded. "If you've done anything to Chris, I'll . . ."

Seth moved so fast that even Talli could barely see him. In less than a second he was standing on the stage, with Donna on her knees before him. "You'll do what?" he sneered. "You'll do nothing. By now your precious little brother is probably dead."

"You're lying!" Donna screamed.

"Am I? In a moment you'll be dead, too. Then you can have a nice little family reunion." His hand snaked out and clamped on to Donna's

179

chin. He drew her to her feet and leaned down as if he were going to kiss her.

"You know," he said softly. "You really are quite lovely." With his free hand, he brushed his fingers through Donna's short brown hair. "I came to this town to bring other golds under my wing. At the moment I have only one new recruit, but I could have two." He looked past her to where Talli stood.

"What do you say, dear?" he asked. "Do you want a new sister?"

Chris clenched the silver knife tight in his hand. "Ready?" he asked.

"I guess," Sky said. She looked down at herself and frowned. "I'd feel better about this if I was myself. But if I was me, I'd never fit in your sister's clothes."

"Just hearing you talk about it makes me dizzy," Chris said. "Maybe you can fool Seth. He'll think you're Donna, and we can use that to our advantage."

"Won't work," she said. "Seth can see by the colors around me that I'm a gold. He'll know it's me."

"Oh." Chris thought for a moment. "Wait a sec," he said. "Maybe you can fool me."

Sky raised her eyebrows. "Now you've lost me."

"You pretend that you've fooled me into thinking that you're Donna," Chris said.

"Okay," Sky said slowly. "And then?"

"And then, when Seth's convinced you're still on his side and he's concentrating on me, you jump him."

She looked at him with a flat expression. "That's your plan?"

Chris shrugged. "You got a better one?"

Sky pursed her lips for a second, then smiled. "I love this plan," she said. "Let's go."

Chris climbed out of the car and followed her across the lawn of Coach Pays's house. He kept his hand jammed down in the pocket of his coat as he walked. The silver knife handle felt slick and sweaty under his fingers. He had killed Casey with a knife just like this one. He would never have done it if she hadn't been attacking Donna, but he *had* done it. He knew a vampire could die. He tried not to think about the fact that Casey was a brand-new, very confused vampire. Even then it hadn't been easy.

Seth would be fast, smart, and strong. If they managed to kill him, it would be more luck than planning. Beyond killing Seth there was something else that frightened Chris even more. What if Seth died and Talli was still a vampire?

I can't afford to worry about that now, he told himself. *Killing Seth is enough to worry about. More than enough.*

Sky reached the door of the house. "Talli's right inside, brother dear," she said loudly. "Come right along, brother. She's dying to see you again." She grabbed the door handle and pulled it open. "Good luck," she mouthed silently as she waved Chris past.

He stepped into the dark living room. In the dim gray light from the door, Chris could see only the dim shapes of furniture. Somewhere deep in the house something clicked, and Chris jumped as the furnace rumbled to life. But except for the soft rush of warm air, everything was quiet and still.

"Uh . . . Donna," he said. "Where is she?"

Sky stepped into the room and turned around slowly. "No one's here," she said. "Sorry. At night I could have told that from outside, but the daylight screws up my sight."

"Where are they?"

"I don't know. They're supposed to meet me on the edge of town at sundown." Sky went back to the door and looked up at the gray winter clouds. "That's about an hour away, but maybe they went out there already."

"I guess we go out there, then," Chris said.

"Before we do, would you mind if I went and changed? Back to myself, I mean." She wrinkled her nose. "I don't want to screw up your plan, but this is really uncomfortable."

"Sure," Chris said. "Get back to yourself. We'll come up with another plan."

"Be with you in a sec." Sky headed out of the room.

Chris found a light switch on the wall and

snapped it on. There were trophies and trophy cases all over the room. On the far wall was a large photo of Casey. Chris walked over to look at it more closely.

In the picture Casey was wearing a sweaty shirt with a large number pinned to the front. Her cheeks were flushed, she held up a shiny trophy, and her face was crossed with the quirky smile that Chris remembered.

"I'm sorry," he whispered to the picture. "I'm really sorry."

He sat down on the couch to wait for Sky. As he sat, he felt something hard beneath him. Chris stood and picked up the slim leather volume that had been lying on the couch. "Westerberg High School," it said along the spine. Chris flipped it open and found that it was the school yearbook. He glanced at several pages, noticing a number of familiar faces.

A cluster of photographs slid out of the book and fluttered to the floor. Chris dropped the yearbook onto the couch and leaned down to pick up the pictures. They were brand-new instant photographs. The first one showed Talli walking in the middle of a crowd of students. Next was a shot of Coach Pays. Then there was a picture of Chris standing in the lunch line.

"What are these?" he called.

"What?" Sky answered.

"These pictures," he said, looking at several

more shots of Talli and himself. "Where did these come from?"

Sky came back into the room. She was once again tall and thin and had no more in common with Chris's sister than eye color. "Man, that feels much better," she said. "I'm too used to being tall to start looking people square in the chin."

Chris held up a handful of the photos. "Where did these come from?" he asked again.

"Oh, those. I took them," Sky said. "Seth went through the local papers the day we arrived and found all the stuff about the missing students. That's why he had me get the yearbook, so he could see what they all looked like. Then he had me take pictures of you and Talli, and the people who weren't in the book. Came in handy for me."

"How was it handy?" Chris asked.

Sky reached into the pile of fallen pictures and pulled out a couple. "That's how I remembered what your sister looked like," she said.

Chris had that painful sinking feeling in his stomach. "You took pictures of Donna and showed them to Seth?"

Sky looked at him and nodded. "Something wrong?"

There was a sharp crack, and the trophy case next to Chris exploded in a shower of glass.

"Get down," Sky shouted as she ran across the room.

Chris was too stunned to respond. Everything was moving very slowly. There was another rippling crack of gunfire. The bullet whirled past in slow motion, coming so close that Chris could feel the hot wind of it passing by his face. The sound of it striking the wall beside his head was like a crash of thunder.

Time suddenly snapped back to normal. Chris dived to the floor and rolled behind a coffee table. The gun boomed twice more. Chris peeked up from behind the table in time to see Sky jerk back as a bullet smashed into her arm. The expression on her beautiful face turned into a snarl, and she leaped through the door. There was yelling, and the sound of struggle. Then rapid footsteps across the snow, the slam of a car door, and the roar of a vehicle pulling away.

Chris climbed cautiously to his knees. "Sky," he called. "Are you okay?" There was no response. The sharp scent of gunpowder lingered in the air as he got to his feet. "Sky?"

"I'm here," she said.

Chris hurried outside and found Sky sitting on the porch. She looked up at him, and he saw shock in her black eyes.

"That maniac shot me," she said.

"Are you all right?"

She nodded. "I will be. I'm almost healed now, but it sure hurt." She stood up and brushed the snow from her black jeans.

"Who was it?" Chris asked.

"Pays," Sky replied. "Your school's football coach. He was planning on shooting you when I first stopped him a couple of nights ago—I was wearing Casey's shape at the time. Seth wanted to keep him around. He talked about having Pays kill you, but I thought he was just saving the man for some extra energy. Guess I was wrong."

"The next time you hear Seth planning a way to take me out, I'd appreciate if you tell me about it," Chris said.

"You got it." Sky flexed her arm, and Chris saw that a long tear ran up the sleeve. "This was one of my best sweaters," she said sadly.

"It's not bad enough I have to go up against vampires," Chris said. "Now you're telling me there's a madman out there who wants to shoot me."

"Everybody has problems," Sky said.

Chris started to make a sharp reply, but he stopped when he saw that Sky was grinning at him. "You have a strange sense of humor," he said. "Come on. Let's get going."

"Where are we going?" she asked.

"To the school," Chris said. He started for the black car.

Sky fell in at his side. "You think Seth is at the school? Why would he be there?"

"Remember, that's where the police said they found Talli's car." He opened the passenger door and hopped inside. "And you showed Seth pic-

186

tures of my sister," he added as Sky got behind the wheel.

"You think Seth would go after your sister?" she asked.

"There's only one way to find out. I want to get over there as fast as possible."

Sky pushed the car quickly through its gears and sent it sliding along the road. "I've been around him for a lot longer than you have, and I don't think he'd do something like that."

"You didn't think he'd send Coach Pays after me with a gun, either, did you?" Chris asked.

"Good point," Sky said. She scowled at the road ahead. "It's starting to snow again."

"Of course it is," Chris replied. "Whatever would be worst for us is what's going to happen."

"I hope you're wrong about that. Seth can think up some pretty bad things."

By the time they reached downtown Westerberg, the snow had become a solid white wall in front of the car. Other cars appeared as dull-white glows and quickly vanished again. The tires of the big car slipped and skidded over the road.

"Can you see through this?" Chris asked.

Sky shook her head. "My eyes are good for a lot, but seeing through blizzards isn't part of the package."

"Why does it always seem like vampires and snow go together?" Chris leaned toward the dashboard and squinted through the curtain of falling flakes.

"Seth probably made it snow," Sky said.

Chris looked at her in surprise. "Seth can control the weather?"

Sky grinned. "No, but it makes a good story, doesn't it?"

She slowed to a crawl as they left the downtown area and started down the long hill toward the school. Twice the rear end of the car started to slip out to the side, and Chris was sure they were about to wreck. But both times Sky twisted hard on the steering wheel and straightened out the car.

"I'm glad you're driving," Chris said after the second near disaster.

"*I'm* not," she said. "I'm scared to death."

"Of having a wreck?"

"Nope, of making it to the school." She shook her hair back from her face. "When we get there, Seth is probably going to make a car wreck look like a party."

According to the clock it was just after five when they reached the school, but it might as well have been midnight. Even the snow looked dark as it threatened to overwhelm the wipers and cover the windshield with ice. Sky guided the car slowly through the drifts that were already moving across the empty parking lot.

"I don't think there's anyone here," she said.

"Wait," Chris said. He wiped the fog from his

window and squinted at the snow. "That's my sister's car. She's still here." His fingers dug into the leather upholstery. "They're all here."

The dark form of the school loomed up out of the snow. Sky drove the car right up onto the sidewalk in front of the door. "Here we are."

"You can stop now," Chris said.

"What do you mean?" she asked.

Chris looked into her black eyes. "You don't have to go in there with me. You can tell Seth that the weather kept you from getting to the airport, and go right back to the way things were before."

She shook her head. "I can't go back. I've been with Seth for a long time, Chris. A lot longer than you might believe. I've tried to get away from him before, but he always brings me back. This time Seth will die or I will. Either way, I'll get out."

Chris opened his door, lowered his head, and forced his way through the wind and snow. He reached the door to the school, but found it locked. He was about to try another when Sky reached past him and snapped it open with one sharp pull.

"There are some things about being a gold I'm going to miss," she said as they stepped in out of the snow.

The long corridors of the school were empty of students and almost completely dark. The only noise was the buzzing of the emergency lights along the ceiling. Chris led the way through the halls to Donna's classroom. He slid the knife from his pocket as he approached the door, but when he stepped into the room, he found it as empty as the rest of the school.

"I was hoping they'd be in here," he said. "We could look in this place for hours without finding them."

"Excuse me," said a voice from behind them.

Chris spun around to find Talli standing in the open classroom door. "Talli! Thank God you're okay." He took a step toward her, but she shied back.

"I came to give an invitation," she said.

Chris looked at her in confusion. "An invitation?"

"What kind of invitation?" Sky asked.

"Seth is waiting," Talli said. "He says come quickly, or he'll kill your sister."

Fifteen

A single spotlight shone down on the stage. In the circle of light Donna stood with her chin tilted back and her eyes looking up to the ceiling. Around her lay the torn canvas and broken boards of a smashed stage set. Outside the light everything was shrouded in darkness.

Chris wanted to run to his sister, but he held back. Seth had as much as announced that this was a trap. "Where is he?" Chris whispered.

"He's waiting for you," Talli said.

Chris looked over at Talli. Her green eyes were wide, but dull. After telling them to come to the auditorium, she hadn't responded to any of Chris's questions. Sky had said that new vampires had problems thinking. That probably accounted for the strange way Talli was acting.

He said a silent prayer. Chris had several theories about why Alex's death hadn't cured Talli. It might have been because Talli wasn't completely a vampire when Alex died. Or it could have been that Alex had really died in the fire, not from what Talli did to him. Or it could have been simply that she was too far away when Alex finally died. The only way to know if Seth's death would cure her was for her to kill Seth. If it didn't work, if Seth's death didn't end all this once and for all, Chris had no idea what to do next.

"Where is he?" he whispered again.

Sky stepped in front of them and looked around. "I can't see Seth," she said. "He's good at hiding his light when he wants to."

Chris took the knife from his pocket and shrugged off his coat. "There's no way to surprise him now, anyway. He's made this trap for us. We might as well go on down there and spring it."

He started down the center aisle toward his sister. Something creaked to his left. Chris whirled around. Nothing. A thump to his right. He spun again in time to see one of the folding seats shaking slightly.

"Seth?" he said softly. He cleared his throat and yelled. "Seth! Come out. I want to talk to you."

In response all the chairs in the auditorium suddenly began to flop up and down. They made a thunderous noise, like a crowd of giants clapping. With a scream of tortured metal, a whole

192

row of seats went crashing over. Deep laughter filled the room, growing even louder than the banging seats.

Chris held the knife high and turned around and around. The laughter always seemed to be at his back. The high curtains at the sides of the stage ripped free and fluttered out over the chairs. Chris had to jump back to avoid the edge of the heavy cloth as it blanketed the ground in dark purple.

Everything stopped. The silence was so sudden and intense that Chris could hear nothing but the blood rushing through his ears.

"Christopher Delany," said a voice high overhead. "How wonderful. Has the fearless vampire hunter come to do in the terrible monster?"

Chris looked up into the shadows above the stage, but there were no lights, and he couldn't see a thing. "Come down, Seth," he called.

There was a long rumbling groan. Something glinted metallically in the air over Donna's head. Something large and heavy. Flecks of plaster and dust drifted downward, glowing like snow in the spotlight.

"Donna!" Chris shouted. He ran toward the stage. "Donna, move!"

With a sharp crack the catwalk above the stage let go. It swept down at Donna like the blade of a huge ax. As Chris vaulted onto the stage, the end of the catwalk sliced through the air inches above his sister's head. With a crash that made the boards under Chris's feet jump, the corner of the catwalk struck the stage three feet to Donna's right.

Ropes still held up one end, and the twisted length of metal rocked and pivoted like a broken swing as its far end dangled high overhead. The severed ends of power cables hung around the dangling mass, sparking and hissing in the air. Through it all Donna didn't move a muscle.

Chris reached her and put his hands on her shoulders. "Donna, are you all right?"

Her head rolled down from her upward gaze. Her mouth opened and closed like a fish pulled from the water, but it was Seth's voice that came out. "Quite the hero, aren't you?"

Chris stumbled back. "Seth? Donna? Who are you?"

Donna's mouth snapped opened and closed again. "It's your luscious sister," said Seth's voice. "I'm just playing puppeteer." Donna took a jerky step forward, holding her hands up like a marionette on strings. "What do you think of my act?"

"Let her go!" Chris shouted. "You're not after her."

"How do you know what I'm after?" asked the voice, but this time it came from darkness overhead.

Like a spider dropping from its web, Seth slid down a rope and landed lightly on the stage next to the slowly rocking wreck of the catwalk.

He still looked like Chris, but the expression on his face was one that Chris had never worn: pure disgust. "All you greens, you think you're so smart. You don't know anything."

Chris put his arm around his sister. He backed away, drawing her with him and waving the knife in the air. "Stay where you are," he said. "This is silver."

"Of course it is," Seth said. He folded his arms across his chest. "Are you ready?" he asked.

Chris kept backing away. "Ready for what?"

Seth disappeared.

Chris had an impression of something moving past him almost as fast as the bullet that had zipped by his face. He started to turn.

"Look out!" Sky yelled.

Then Chris was flying. He arched high over the stage, just missing the edge of the dangling catwalk. He was just starting to extend his hands when the boards came up and slapped him in the face. The blow knocked the breath out of Chris and left stars swirling through his vision. He rolled over and got to his knees. Wheezing and coughing, he looked up to see Donna lying in a heap at the edge of the stage and his own sneering face looking down at him.

"I kill every night," said the thing with Chris's face. "Sometimes several times a night." He curled his fingers, clawlike, before him and looked down at them as if he were examining his nails. Slowly, the ends of his fingers

195

stretched and curved into bone-white claws. "But I rarely get the opportunity to enjoy a kill this much."

A boom resounded through the auditorium. The front of Seth's sweater exploded outward in a spray of electricity and gore. His eyes widened in surprise. Before he could turn, there was another boom, and a bullet carved a groove through the side of his head.

Willard Pays climbed onto the stage with his gun held out in front of him. His eyes flashed with an inner fire as he walked slowly forward.

Seth pivoted toward him. Like a man walking into a stiff wind, he walked to Coach Pays through a stream of bullets that smashed into his chest, his head, his arms. Each bullet that struck him released a ray of brilliant white light. It made Chris think of someone punching holes in a lamp shade. Seth's wounds shone radiantly in the dark auditorium. He was almost too bright to look at.

The rolling echo of Pays's shots died away, and there was a final click as he pulled the trigger on an empty chamber. "That's for my Casey," he said.

Seth reached out and snatched the gun from his hand. "You great bloody fool!" he thundered.

With his other hand he struck Pays a blow to the head that lifted the tall man from his feet. The coach fell limply to the stage, dark blood leaking from his nose and ears.

Chris recovered his breath and got to his knees. He had lost the knife when Seth hurled him across the stage. He had to find the knife. It was the only thing that could save them. He scrambled through the pieces of canvas and wood that littered the stage, searching for the gleam of silver.

Seth gave a thin, wordless cry that caught Chris's attention. The vampire stood stiffly, with his arms stretched out to the side and his clawed hands curled into trembling knots. Snakes of blue light twisted and smoked around him. The shining wounds caused by the bullets shrank quickly to brilliant pinpoints, then vanished.

Seth's features were no longer an imitation of Chris's. They were no longer even human. His nose was a twisted mass of purple flesh that made Chris think of a bat. His eyes were pits of red fire. "That hurt," he said in a voice deep as thunder. His mouth was a twisted gash filled with curving needles for teeth. He stepped toward Chris on warped, twisted legs and reached for him with hands that were nests of curving blades.

A lean figure sprang onto the stage. "Over here," Sky called.

The misshapen form turned, its gaping mouth forming a horrible parody of Seth's usual smile. "Sky," it rumbled. "You picked the wrong time to betray me."

Without another word Sky leaped at him.

Seth's distorted arms went around her as the impact toppled him. The two figures rolled across the stage in a tangle of limbs. As the vampires fought, Chris kicked aside the debris at his feet. He turned up boards, nails, and yellowed scripts, but there was no sign of the lost knife.

With a howl of triumph Seth stood. His hands were tight around Sky's neck, and he shook her like a rag. "You shouldn't have tried it, little Sky," he growled.

"Fifty years," she choked out. "Fifty years of letting you bully me. That's enough."

Waves of pale light washed over Seth. With the passage of each wave he became more human, until he again looked like the young man Chris and Talli had met in the cemetery. "Fifty years," he said thoughtfully. Like his face, his voice was back to normal. "Has it been that long?"

Sky nodded.

Seth smiled at his fellow vampire. "You're right, Sky. That's long enough." He took his hands off her neck and moved them to her shoulders.

"You're going to let me go?" she asked.

"Certainly," Seth replied. "I'll let you go." He tilted his head to the side and looked at her with a tender smile. "I'll let you go the moment you're dead."

There was a sharp crack as her shoulder bones broke under his grip. Sky screamed as

Seth pressed even harder. Liquid light pulsed from her wounds and splashed onto the stage. Sky's scream rose in pitch until Chris could no longer hear it. Sparks played along her teeth, and smoke curled out of her brown hair. Seth lifted her high over his head, gripping her feet with one hand and her neck with the other. With a sharp jerk he broke her back like a dry twig. Then he tossed her far out into the seats. "Good-bye, dear Sky," he said. "It was a fine fifty years."

He turned back to Chris, his maddening smile still firmly fixed on his face. "Now, where were we?"

Chris spotted the knife. He leaped for it, rolled behind the broken catwalk, and came up with the blade pointed at Seth. "We were about to kill you," he said.

Seth threw back his head and laughed. "This is even more fun than I thought it would be." Still chuckling, he started across the stage.

Chris looked up into the tangle of ropes and cables that hung down around the dangling catwalk. Most of the ropes were slack in fact, only one still seemed to be attached to the upper end of the catwalk. Quickly, Chris traced its path up into the darkness, and back down to a tie off right at his elbow. Without even stopping to see where Seth was, Chris slashed at the rope with his knife.

The rope snapped at the first touch of the

blade. Chris turned just in time to see thirty feet of planks, metal pipes, and sandbags come crashing down as the catwalk fell onto Seth. Chris walked toward the wreckage with his knife held ready. Nothing could be seen of Seth except one bare arm sticking out from under a pile of twisted metal. As Chris watched, the hand began to move, pushing aside pipes and broken boards. Chris knelt and raised the knife. Then he looked for Talli. If he struck now, she might be too far away for Seth's death to help her. In fact, Chris didn't know if Talli would be cured unless she was the one to deliver the killing blow. Chris opened his mouth to call for her.

Seth exploded out of the wreckage. A back-handed slap struck Chris's forearm so hard that he heard the snap of his breaking bones. The knife dropped from his numb fingers.

Seth rose up over him. The vampire's face was a ruin of torn flesh. There was exposed bone down the side of his face, and a gaping wound in his chest showed a curving length of gleaming rib. Dribbles of liquid light rolled around the wounds. His eyes were alive with rage.

"When are you going to give up and die, Chris?" he asked. His torn lips curled in an infuriating smile.

Chris glanced to his left. "Not quite yet," he replied. He grabbed an electric cable from the ground and shoved its exposed end into the hole in Seth's chest.

Seth screamed. Oily smoke poured from his open mouth. He reached to pull the cable from his chest, but before he could get a grip, the flesh withered from his arms, and he shrank to a skeleton wrapped in charred skin. The skeleton fell back against the stage with a sound that was almost musical.

"Silver. Salt water. All that talk about energy." Chris did his best to imitate Seth's smile and superior tone. "I had a hunch you wouldn't care for electricity, Seth."

He stood, swaying from sudden exhaustion, and staggered to where Donna lay. She was breathing. Chris closed his eyes and gave a silent moment of thanks. Donna was alive, and that was worth almost anything. He glanced out into the seats below and saw Talli looking up at him. Her eyes still looked glazed, and her expression was blank. Chris's heart sank. He had acted to save his own life, but at the critical moment, he had forgotten Talli.

"Talli," Chris said, "are you still—"

Hard fingers closed around Chris's throat, cutting off his words and lifting him from his sister's side. With deliberate slowness he was turned to face a blackened skull. "Not quite enough," Seth said. His voice was like the hiss of dry leaves in December. "It was a good try, but not quite enough. Now I kill you." The skull turned slightly, the empty eye sockets pointed over Chris's shoulder. "On second thought,"

Seth added, "I'll let my new assistant do it."

Talli McAlister stepped to Seth's side. "You shouldn't have tried to hurt him," she said. "He's important to me."

"Talli," Chris gasped. "I only wanted—" He choked as Seth tightened his bony grip.

Talli raised her hand, and Chris saw that she had the silver knife in her grip. Sparks trailed over her fingers, and the skin of her hand was blistered and red. "You shouldn't have tried to hurt him," she repeated.

Seth gave a dry laugh. "Killed with his own weapon," he hissed. "How appropriate."

Talli swung around and drove the silver knife completely through Seth's thin neck. The blackened skull flew across the stage and shattered into a thousand fragments as it struck the boards. For a long moment the headless skeleton stood, its fleshless fingers still wrapped around Chris's neck. Then the bones fell apart and crumbled into a shapeless pile.

"I told you you shouldn't have hurt him," Talli said. She threw down the knife, flung her arms around Chris, and pulled him into a painfully tight hug. "He's very important to me."

A distant humming sound began in the air over the stage. It rose quickly to an earsplitting shriek. Bolts of lightning shot down and left smoking pits in the boards. Then there was a flash as bright as a thousand lightbulbs. When Chris could see again, the lightning was gone, and so was all sign of Seth.

"I can't see!" Talli cried.

"That flash was bright," Chris said. "You'll probably be okay in a second."

Talli shook her head. "I can see," she said. "I just can't *see*. I mean, I can't see the glow around you. Chris, I think I'm back to normal." She squeezed him again.

Chris grinned. "I knew my theory would work."

Talli looked puzzled. "What theory?"

"Never mind," he said. "The important thing is, you're okay. And if you're okay . . ." He pulled away from Talli and ran to the edge of the stage. "Sky! Are you back to normal?"

He jumped down to the foot of the stage, and stumbled as his broken arm banged against his side, sending a searing jolt of pain all through his body. Then he ran up into the seats to where Seth had flung his rebellious companion.

Sky was crumpled on the floor. There didn't seem to be an intact bone in her body. Even her skull was flat on one side from the force of her impact with the hard floor.

Chris's voice caught in his throat. "Sky?" he croaked.

Her black eyes flickered open. "Is he dead?" she whispered.

He nodded. "He's gone. Are you still a vampire?"

"Yes." She started to sit up, but fell back hard

against the floor. "Help me," she groaned.

He knelt on the cold floor and took her hand. "How?"

"I need to feed," she said. "I've got to have more energy to heal."

"Take it from me," Chris said.

She shook her head the tiniest bit. "I need too much. It would kill you."

"Then take some from me, too." Talli knelt down beside Chris. "You helped me," she said. "Now it's my turn."

Sky looked at her for a long moment. "You're a green again. You turned."

Talli nodded.

Sky opened her mouth, then shut it again. "I guess I'm glad I'm not, because I'd probably be dead."

A few minutes later Sky looked like herself again, and Chris felt even more exhausted. While Sky fed carefully from Talli, Chris went to the stage and sat down beside his sister. "Donna?" He shook her gently. "You in there?"

She rolled over and opened one eye. "Chris?" She propped herself up on an elbow and looked at him for a second. "You're wearing that ratty old green sweater again."

"Yeah," Chris said. "Is that important right now?"

She grinned tiredly. "It is to me."

Suddenly the auditorium was flooded with light as the banks of fixtures overhead snapped on. A door creaked at the rear of the rows of seats, and a thin figure loomed up out of the shadows. Chris looked around desperately, wondering what had become of the knife.

Officer Lansky stepped out into the light. "What the devil happened in here?" he asked.

Sixteen

"So it was Willard Pays who was driving your car?"

"That's right," Talli said.

Sergeant Lansky shut his notebook. "And Pays who kidnapped Donna Delany, and almost destroyed the school, and tried to shoot you, and shot up his own house. Is that right?"

"That's pretty much it," Chris said. He adjusted the sling around his arm. "Can we stop now? We've answered all your questions ten times."

Lansky stood up. "Yes, you have," he said, "and I don't believe your answers any more now than I did the first time." He shoved his pen into his shirt pocket. "But the chief believes them, and Sergeant McAlister believes them, and I suppose in this Podunk town that's what matters."

He picked up his coat. "So I'll get out of your house, Mr. Delany. I expect this case will be closed quickly. We'll let you know if we need anything more." He turned and headed for the door.

"What about Casey Pays's disappearance?" Chris called after him.

Lansky stopped. "Funny you should ask about that." He turned slowly. "It seems that a young woman identified as Ms. Casey Leah Pays entered the Stroud City police station this morning."

"That's great!" Talli said.

"Is she coming home?" Chris asked.

"We don't know," Lansky said. "The young lady said she had left Westerberg to get away from her father. The officers attempted to retain her long enough for someone from Westerberg to talk to her, but she somehow managed to slip away."

"I'm sorry to hear that," Chris said, "but I guess that means we're not under investigation for Casey's disappearance."

"Yes," he said. "I guess it does." Lansky slammed the door on his way out.

Talli slid across the couch and put her arms around Chris. "It's over," she said.

He nodded. "I guess it is. I'm really sorry about Coach Pays. First he lost Casey, then Seth kills him, and now he's taking the blame for everything. If I could figure out another way . . ."

"I'm sorry, too. But if he hadn't been trying to kill us, he would never have gotten mixed up in this. It's a miracle that more people aren't dead," Talli said. "Just be thankful things turned out the way they did."

The doorbell rang. Chris winced. "The police may have closed the case, but it looks like we're still Grand Central Station."

"Stay here. I'll get it." Talli hurried to the door and found Sky standing on the doorstep.

"Are you going to ask me in?" she said. "Otherwise, I'm stuck."

Talli smiled. "Get in here."

Sky strolled past her into the living room. Already Talli could see something different in the way Sky moved. She was more confident, smoother. It was if Seth's destruction was finally allowing Sky to grow up.

"Thanks for the favor this morning," Chris said.

Sky bowed. "No problem. Casey Pays was tall. Playing her wasn't as tough as it was being a pip-squeak like your sister."

"I heard that!" came a voice from the next room. Donna popped through the door and waved a pencil at her. "You're a height bigot," she said. Then she marched back through the door.

Sky turned around. "I think she hears better than Seth did."

"She's a teacher," Chris said. "All teachers have bionic ears."

"It's been a long time since I've been in school," Sky said, "but I seem to remember that." She shifted uncomfortably. "Well, I guess I'll be going."

"Where will you go?" Talli asked.

Sky shrugged. "I don't know. It's been so long since I made a decision on my own, I might go anywhere."

"Why don't you stay here for a while?" Chris asked. "You're welcome to stay with us."

Talli looked at him and frowned. "I'm not sure I like that idea too much. Not that I don't like Sky. I'm just not sure I want you two in the same house."

"Thanks for the offer," Sky said, "but I don't want to take the chance. Seth was telling the truth—we can live on just a little bit of energy from a lot of people. But it's hard to keep it under control. I don't want to be in Westerberg if things get out of hand." She looked at Chris, then Talli. "There are people here I care about."

Sky walked over and gave Chris a quick kiss that left him blinking in surprise. "You take care of Talli," she said.

"I will."

Then she walked over to Talli and wrapped her long arms around the smaller girl in a tight hug.

"Careful," Talli said. "I'm not as strong as I used to be."

Sky released her. "Watch out for this guy,"

she said with a nod toward Chris. "He must be crazy to go as far as he did for you."

"I know," Talli said. "Is there anything we can do for you?"

A wide grin came to Sky's face. "If you ever decide you don't want Chris . . ."

"I don't know," Chris said. "I've never thought much about older women."

Sky rolled her eyes. "While you're watching out for him," she said to Talli, "try to teach him some manners, okay?"

"I'll try," Talli said, "but it may be hopeless."

"In the meantime," Sky said, "I think I'll see if I can find another vampire."

"Why?" Chris asked.

"There are a lot of them out there just as nasty as Seth," Sky said. "I think I'll give your theory another try."

"But I thought Seth made you," Talli said. "Maybe I was cured only because Seth was the one that turned me. What if you kill one of them and it doesn't work?"

"Then I'll know. And at least the world will be rid of one more bad vampire." Sky went to the door, gave a quick wave, and was gone.

Talli sat down on the couch beside Chris. For a long time they just leaned against each other and enjoyed the silence.

ABOUT THE AUTHOR

M. C. Sumner lives out in the country, in a town even smaller than Westerberg. His house is perched precariously on the side of a hill, and he is the proud owner of one of the ugliest patches of woods in several states. Like many writers, he keeps a menagerie of animals, with current residents that include an iguana, a giant day gecko, an African house snake, a tank of fish, several mice, and one very spoiled golden retriever.

In addition to this trilogy and his previous book, *Deadly Stranger*, he has sold a number of short stories. His stories have appeared in *Isaac Asimov's Science Fiction* magazine, *Tomorrow* magazine, *Dragon* magazine, and in a number of anthologies. He was a first-place winner in the Writers of the Future Contest.

He is currently at work on a new crop of young adult thrillers.

■ HarperPaperbacks *By Mail*

Read all of L. J. Smith's spine-tingling thrillers.

This new series from the bestselling author of The Vampire Diaries tells the thrilling story of Cassie, who makes a startling discovery when she moves to New Salem: She is the last of a long line of witches. Now she must seize her power or lose it forever. . . .

THE VAMPIRE DIARIES
by L.J. Smith

The romantic, terrifying chronicle of a dark love triangle: two vampire brothers and the beautiful girl who's torn between them.

Volume I: THE AWAKENING

Volume II: THE STRUGGLE

Volume III: THE FURY

Volume IV: THE REUNION

Look for: **TEEN IDOL** *by Kate Daniel*

Volume I: THE INITIATION
Volume II: THE CAPTIVE
Volume III: THE POWER

- - - - - - - - - - - - - - - - - -